Andersen's Fairy Tales

HANS CHRISTIAN ANDERSEN

WEEKLY READER BOOKS

This book is a presentation of
Weekly Reader Books.

Weekly Reader Books offers
several exciting card
and activity programs.

For further information write to:
Weekly Reader Books
1250 Fairwood Ave.
Columbus, Ohio 43216

Cover illustration by Richard Moss
Text illustrations by Dick Smolinski

Printed in U.S.A.

CONTENTS

"You shall have as much money as ever you like," the old witch told the soldier.

The Tinder Box

A soldier came marching along the highroad. One, two! One, two! He had his knapsack on his back and his sword at his side, for he had been to the wars and now he was on his way home. He met an old witch on the road. She was so ugly that her lower lip hung right down onto her chin.

She said, "Good evening, soldier! What a nice sword you've got, and such a big knapsack. You are a real soldier! You shall have as much money as ever you like."

"Thank you kindly, you old witch," said the soldier.

"Do you see that big tree?" said the witch, pointing to a tree close by. "It is hollow inside. Climb up to the top and you will see a hole into which you can let yourself down, right down under the tree. I will tie a rope round your waist so that I can haul you up again when you call."

"What am I to do down under the tree?" asked the soldier.

"Fetch money," said the witch. "You must know that when you get down to the bottom of the tree you will find yourself in a wide passage. It's quite light there, for there are over a hundred blazing lamps. You will see three doors which you can open, for the keys are there. If you go into the first room you will see a big box in the middle of the floor. A dog is sitting on the top of it and he has eyes as big as saucers, but you needn't mind that. I will give you my blue-checked apron, which you can spread out on the floor. Go quickly forward, take up the dog, and put him on my apron. Then open the box and take out as much money as you like. It is all copper, but if you like silver better, go into the next room. There you will find a dog with eyes as big as millstones. But never mind that. Put him on my apron and take the money. If you prefer gold you can have it too, and as much as you can carry, if you go into the third room. But the dog sitting on that box has eyes each as big as the Round Tower. He *is* a dog, indeed, as you may imagine. But don't let it trouble you. You only have to put him on my apron. Then he won't hurt you, and you can take as much gold out of the box as you like! "

"That's not so bad," said the soldier. "But what am I to give you, old witch? You'll want something, I'll be bound."

"No," said the witch. "Not a single penny do I want. I only want you to bring me an old tinder box that my grandmother forgot the last time she was down there."

"Well, tie the rope round my waist," said the soldier.

"Here it is," said the witch. "And here is my blue-checked apron."

Then the soldier climbed up the tree, let himself slide down the hollow trunk, and found himself, as the witch had said, in the wide passage where the many hundred lamps were burning.

Now he opened the first door. Ugh! There sat the dog with eyes as big as saucers staring at him.

"You are a nice fellow! " said the soldier, as he put him onto the witch's apron and took out as many pennies as he could cram into his pockets. Then he shut the box, put the dog on the top of it again, and went into the next room. Hallo! There sat the dog with eyes as big as millstones.

"You shouldn't stare at me so hard. You might get a pain in your eyes! " Then he put the dog on the apron, but when he saw all the silver in the box he threw away all the coppers and stuffed his pockets and his knapsack with silver. Then he went into the third room. Oh, how horrible! That dog really had two eyes as big as the Round Tower, and they rolled around and around like wheels.

"Good evening," said the soldier, saluting, for he had never seen such a dog in his life. But after looking at him for a bit he thought, "That will do." And then he lifted him down onto the apron and opened the chest. Heavens! What a lot of gold! He could buy the whole of Copenhagen with it, and all the sugar pigs from the cake-woman, all the tin soldiers, whips, and rocking horses in the world. That was money indeed! Now the soldier threw away all the silver he had filled his pockets and his knapsack with and put gold in its place. Yes, he crammed all his pockets, his knapsack, his cap, and his boots so full that he could hardly walk. Now, he really had got a lot of money. He put the dog back onto the box, shut the door, and shouted up through the tree, "Haul me up, you old witch!"

"Have you got the tinder box?"

"Oh, to be sure!" said the soldier. "I had quite forgotten it." And he went back to fetch it. The witch hauled him up, and there he was standing on the highroad again with his pockets, boots, knapsack, and cap full of gold.

"What do you want the tinder box for?" asked the soldier.

"That's no business of yours," said the witch. "You've got the money. Give me the tinder box!"

"Rubbish!" said the soldier. "Tell me directly what you want with it or I will draw my sword and cut off your head."

"I won't!" said the witch.

Then the soldier cut off her head. There she lay! But he tied all the money up in her apron, slung it on his back like a pack, put the tinder box in his pocket, and marched off to the town.

It was a beautiful town. He went straight to the finest hotel and ordered the grandest rooms and all the food he liked best, because he was a rich man now that he had so much money.

Certainly the servant who had to clean his boots thought they were funny old things for such a rich gentleman, but he had not had time yet to buy any new ones. The next day he bought new boots and fine clothes. The soldier now became a fine gentleman, and the people told him all about the grand things in the town, and about their king, and what a lovely princess his daughter was.

"Where is she to be seen?" asked the soldier.

"You can't see her at all," they all said. "She lives in a great copper castle surrounded with walls and towers. Nobody but the King dares to go in and out, for it has been prophesied that she will marry a common soldier, and the King doesn't like that!"

"I should like to see her well enough," thought the soldier. But there was no way of getting leave for that.

He now led a very merry life. He went to theatres, drove about in the King's Park, and gave away a lot of money to poor people, which was very nice of him. He remembered how disagreeable it used to be not to have a penny in his pocket. Now he was rich, wore fine clothes, and had a great many friends who all said what a nice fellow he was— a thorough gentleman—and he liked to be told that.

But as he went on spending money every day and his store was never renewed, he at last found himself with only two pence left. Then he was obliged to move out of his fine rooms. He had to take a tiny little attic up under the roof, clean his own boots, and mend them himself with a darning needle. None of his friends went to see him because there were far too many stairs.

One dark evening when he had not even enough money to buy a candle with, he suddenly remembered that there was a little bit in the old tinder box he had brought out of the hollow tree, when the witch helped him down. He got

out the tinder box with the candle end in it and struck fire.
But as the sparks flew out from the flint, the door burst
open and the dog with eyes as big as saucers, which he had
seen down under the tree, stood before him and said, "What
does my lord command?"

"By heaven!" said the soldier, "this is a nice kind of
tinder box, if I can get whatever I want like this. Get me
some money," he said to the dog, and away it went.

It was back in a twinkling with a bag full of pennies in
its mouth.

Now the soldier saw what a treasure he had in the tinder
box. If he struck once, the dog which sat on the box of
copper came. If he struck twice, the dog on the silver box
came. And if he struck three times, the one from the box
of gold.

He now moved down to the grand rooms and got his fine
clothes again, and then all his friends knew him once more
and liked him as much as ever.

Then he suddenly began to think, "After all, it's a curious
thing that no man can get a sight of the Princess. Everyone
says she is so beautiful! But what is the good of that when
she always has to be shut up in that big copper palace with
all the towers. Can I not somehow manage to see her?
Where is my tinder box?" Then he struck the flint and,
whisk! came the dog with eyes as big as saucers.

"It certainly is the middle of the night," said the soldier,
"but I am very anxious to see the Princess, if only for a
single moment."

The dog was out of the door in an instant, and before
the soldier had time to think about it, he was back again
with the Princess. There she was, fast asleep on the dog's
back, and she was so lovely that anybody could see that
she must be a real princess. The soldier could not help it,
but he was obliged to kiss her, for he was a true soldier.

Then the dog ran back again with the Princess, but in the

morning, when the King and Queen were having breakfast, the Princess said that she had such a wonderful dream about a dog and a soldier. She had ridden on the dog's back and the soldier had kissed her.

"That's a pretty tale," said the Queen.

After this an old lady-in-waiting had to sit by her bed at night to see if this was really a dream, or what it could be.

The soldier longed so intensely to see the Princess again that at night the dog came to fetch her. He took her up and ran off with her as fast as he could, but the old lady-in-waiting put on her galoshes and ran just as fast behind them. When she saw that they disappeared into a large house, she thought, "Now I know where it is," and made a big cross with chalk on the gate. Then she went home and lay down, and presently the dog came back with the Princess. When he saw that there was a cross on the gate, he took a bit of chalk, too, and made crosses on all the gates in the town. Now this was very clever of him, for the lady-in-waiting could not possibly find the gate when there were crosses on all the gates.

Early next morning the King, the Queen, the lady-in-waiting, and all the court officials went to see where the Princess had been.

"There it is," said the King, when he saw the first door with the cross on it.

"No, my dear husband, it is there," said the Queen, who saw another door with a cross on it.

"But there is one! And there is another!" they all cried out.

They soon saw that it was hopeless to try to find it.

Now the Queen was a very clever woman. She knew more than how to drive in a chariot. She took her big gold scissors and cut up a large piece of silk into small pieces, and made a pretty little bag which she filled with fine grains of buckwheat. She then tied it onto the back of the Princess.

And when that was done she cut a little hole in the bag, so that the grains could drop out all the way wherever the Princess went.

At night the dog came again, took the Princess on his back, and ran off with her to the soldier, who was so fond of her that he longed to be a prince, so that he might have her for his wife.

The dog never noticed how the grain dropped out all along the road from the palace to the soldier's window, where he ran up the wall with the Princess.

In the morning the King and the Queen easily saw where their daughter had been, and they seized the soldier and threw him into the dungeons.

There he lay. Oh, how dark and tiresome it was! And then one day they said to him, "Tomorrow you are to be hanged." It was not amusing to be told that, especially as he had left his tinder box behind him at the hotel.

In the morning he could see through the bars in the little window that the people were hurrying out of the town to see him hanged. He heard the drums and saw the soldiers marching along. All the world was going. Among them was a shoemaker's boy in his leather apron and slippers. He was in such a hurry that he lost one of his slippers, and it fell close under the soldier's window where he was peeping out through the bars.

"I say, you boy! Don't be in such a hurry," said the soldier to him. "Nothing will happen till I get there. But if you will run to the house where I used to live and fetch me my tinder box, you shall have a penny. You must put your best foot foremost."

The boy was only too glad to have the penny and tore off to get the tinder box. He gave it to the soldier and—yes, now we shall hear.

Outside the town a high scaffold had been raised, and the soldiers were drawn up round about it as well as crowds of the townspeople. The King and the Queen sat upon a beautiful throne exactly opposite the judge and all the councilors.

The soldier mounted the ladder, but when they were about to put the rope round his neck, he said that before undergoing his punishment a criminal was always allowed the gratification of a harmless wish, and he wanted very much to smoke a pipe as it would be his last in this world.

The King would not deny him this, so the soldier took out his tinder box and struck fire, once, twice, three times. And there were all the dogs—the one with eyes like saucers, the one with eyes like millstones, and the one whose eyes were as big as the Round Tower.

"Help me! Save me from being hanged," cried the soldier.

And then the dogs rushed at the soldiers and the councilors. They took one by the legs and another by the nose and threw them up many fathoms into the air, and when they fell down they were broken all to pieces.

"I won't!" cried the King, but the biggest dog took both him and the Queen and threw them after all the others. Then the soldiers became alarmed, and the people shouted, "Oh, good soldier, you shall be our King and marry the beautiful Princess!"

Then they conducted the soldier to the King's chariot, and all three dogs danced along in front of him and shouted "Hurrah!" The boys all put their fingers in their mouths and whistled, and the soldiers presented arms. The Princess came out of the copper palace and became Queen, which pleased her very much. The wedding took place in a week, and the dogs all had seats at the table, where they sat staring with all their eyes.

The Princess on the Pea

There was once a Prince who wanted to marry a Princess; but she was to be a *real* princess. So he traveled about, all through the world, to find a real one, but everywhere there was something in the way. There were princesses enough, but whether they were *real* princesses he could not quite make out: there was always something that did not seem quite right. So he came home again, and was quite sad: for he wished so much to have a real princess.

One evening a terrible storm came on. It lightened and thundered, the rain streamed down; it was quite fearful! Then there was a knocking at the town gate, and the old King went out to open it.

It was a Princess who stood outside the gate. But, mercy! how she looked, from the rain and the rough weather! The water ran down from her hair and her clothes; it ran in at the points of her shoes, and out at the heels; and yet she declared that she was a real princess.

"Yes, we will soon find that out," thought the old Queen. But she said nothing, only went into the bedchamber, took all the bedding off, and put a pea on the flooring of the bedstead; then she took twenty mattresses and laid them upon the pea, and then twenty eider-down beds upon the mattresses. On this the Princess had to lie all night. In the morning she was asked how she slept.

The Queen had a most unusual way to find out if the young girl was a real princess or not.

"O, miserably!" said the Princess. "I scarcely closed my eyes all night long. Goodness knows what was in my bed. I lay upon something hard, so that I am black and blue all over. It is quite dreadful!"

Now they saw that she was a real princess, for through the twenty mattresses and the twenty eider-down beds she had felt the pea. No one but a real princess could be so delicate.

So the Prince took her for his wife, for now he knew that he had a true princess; and the pea was put in the museum, and it is there now, unless somebody has carried it off.

Look you, this is a true story.

The Traveling Companion

Poor John was very sad; for his father was very ill, and just dying. There was no one but the two in the little room, and the lamp had nearly burned out; for it was late in the night.

"You have been a good son, John," said the sick father, "and God will help you on in the world." He looked at him, as he spoke, with mild, earnest eyes, drew a deep sigh, and died; yet it appeared as if he still slept.

John wept bitterly. He had no one in the wide world now; neither father, mother, brother, nor sister. Poor John! he knelt down by the bed, kissed his dead father's hand, and wept many, many bitter tears; but at last his eyes closed, and he fell asleep with his head resting against the hard bedpost.

Then he dreamed a strange dream: he thought he saw the sun shining upon him, and his father alive and well, and even heard him laughing as he used to do when he was very happy. A beautiful girl, with a golden crown on her head, and long, shining hair, gave him her hand; and his father said, "See what a bride you have won. She is the loveliest maiden on the whole earth." Then he awoke, and all the beautiful things vanished before his eyes, his father lay dead on the bed, and he was all alone. Poor John!

The week after, the dead man was buried. John walked

behind the coffin which contained his father, whom he so dearly loved, and would never again see. He heard the earth fall on the coffin-lid, and watched it till only a corner remained in sight, and at last also disappeared. He felt as if his heart would break with its weight of sorrow, till those who stood round the grave sang a psalm, and the sweet, holy tones brought tears into his eyes, which relieved him. The sun shone brightly down on the green trees, as if it would say, "You must not be so sorrowful, John. Do you see the beautiful blue sky above you? Your father is up there, and he prays to the loving Father of all, that you may do well in the future."

"I will always be good," said John, "and then I shall go to be with my father in heaven. What joy it will be when we see each other again! How much I shall have to relate to him, and how many things he will be able to explain to me of the delights of heaven, and teach me as he once did on earth. Oh, what joy it will be! "

John pictured it all so plainly to himself, that he smiled even while the tears ran down his cheeks.

The little birds in the chestnut trees twittered, " Tweet, tweet "; they were so happy, although they had seen the funeral; but they seemed as if they knew that the dead man was now in heaven, and that he had wings much larger and more beautiful than their own; that he was happy now, because he had been good here on earth, and they were glad of it. John saw them fly away out of the green trees into the wide world, and he longed to fly with them; but first he cut out a large wooden cross, to place on his father's grave; and when he brought it there in the evening, he found the grave decked out with gravel and flowers. Strangers had done this—they who had known the good old father who was now dead, and who had loved him very much.

Early the next morning, John packed up his little bundle of clothes, and placed all his money, which consisted of

fifty dollars and a few shillings, in his girdle; with this he
determined to try his fortune in the world. But first he
went into the church yard; and, by his father's grave, he
said " Our Father "; and then added: " Farewell, dear father;
I will always be a true and good man, and do thou ask the
good God to make me good."

And as he passed through the fields, all the flowers looked
fresh and beautiful in the warm sunshine, and nodded in
the wind, as if they wished to say, " Welcome to the green
wood; here all is fresh and bright."

Then John turned to have one more look at the old
church, in which he had been christened in his infancy, and
where his father had taken him every Sunday to hear the
service and join in singing the psalms. As he looked at the
old tower, he espied the ringer standing at one of the
narrow openings, with his little pointed red cap on his head,
and shading his eyes from the sun with his bent arm. John
nodded farewell to him; and the little ringer waved his red
cap, laid his hand on his heart, and kissed his hand to him
a great many times, to show that he felt kindly towards him,
and wished him a prosperous journey.

John continued his journey, and thought of all the
wonderful things he should see in the large, beautiful world,
till he found himself farther away from home than ever he
had been before. He did not even know the names of the
places he passed through, and could scarcely understand the
language of the people he met, for he was far away in a
strange land. The first night he slept on a haystack, out in
the fields, for there was no other bed for him; but it seemed
to him so nice and comfortable that even a king need not
wish for a better. The field, the brook, the haystack, with
the blue sky above, formed a beautiful bedroom. The green
grass, with the little red and white flowers, was the carpet;
the elder bushes and the hedges of wild roses looked like
garlands on the walls; and for a bath he could have the

clear, fresh water of the brook; while the rushes bowed their
heads to him, to wish him good morning and good evening.
The moon, like a large lamp, hung high up in the blue ceiling,
and he had no fear of its setting fire to his curtains. John
slept here quite safely all night; and when he awoke, the
sun was up, and all the little birds were singing round him,
"Good morning! good morning! Are you not up yet?"

It was Sunday, and the bells were ringing for church.
As the people went in, John followed them; he heard God's
word, joined in singing the psalms, and listened to the
preacher. It seemed to him just as if he were in his own
church, where he had been christened, and had sung the
psalms with his father. Out in the churchyard were several
graves, and on some of them the grass had grown very high.
John thought of his father's grave, which he knew at last
would look like these, as he was not there to weed and
attend to it. Then he set to work, pulled up the high grass,
raised the wooden crosses which had fallen down, and
replaced the wreaths which had been blown away from their
places by the wind, thinking all the time, "Perhaps some
one is doing the same for my father's grave, as I am not
there to do it."

Outside the churchyard door stood an old beggar, leaning
on his crutch. John gave him his silver shillings, and then
he continued his journey, feeling lighter and happier than
ever. Towards evening, the weather became very stormy,
and he hastened on as quickly as he could, to get shelter:
but it was quite dark by the time he reached a little lonely
church which stood on a hill. "I will go in here," he said,
"and sit down in a corner; for I am quite tired, and want
rest."

So he went in, and seated himself; then he folded his hands,
and offered up his evening prayer, and was soon fast asleep
and dreaming, while the thunder rolled and the lightning
flashed without. When he awoke, it was still night; but the

storm had ceased, and the moon shone in upon him through
the windows. Then he saw an open coffin standing in the
center of the church, which contained a dead man, waiting
for burial. John was not at all timid; he had a good
conscience, and he knew also that the dead can never injure
anyone. It is living, wicked men who do harm to others.
Two such wicked persons stood now by the dead man, who
had been brought to the church to be buried. Their evil
intentions were to throw the poor dead body outside the
church door, and not leave him to rest in his coffin.

"Why do you do this?" asked John, when he saw what
they were going to do; "it is very wicked. Leave him to
rest in peace, in Christ's name."

"Bosh!" replied the two dreadful men. "He has cheated
us; he owed us money which he could not pay, and now
he is dead we shall not get a penny; so we mean to have
our revenge, and let him lie like a dog outside the church
door."

"I have only fifty dollars," said John; "it is all I own in
the world, but I will give it to you if you will promise me
faithfully to leave the dead man in peace. I shall be able to
get on without the money; I have strong and healthy limbs,
and God will always help me."

"Why, of course," said the horrid men, "if you will pay
his debt we will both promise not to touch him. You may
depend upon that"; and then they took the money he offered
them, laughed at him for his good nature, and went their
way.

Then he laid the dead body back in the coffin, folded the
hands, and took leave of it; and went away contentedly
through the great forest. All around him he could see the
prettiest little elves dancing in the moonlight, which shone
through the trees. They were not disturbed by his appearance,
for they knew he was good and harmless among men. They
are wicked people only who can never obtain a glimpse of

fairies. Some of them were not taller than the breadth of a finger, and they wore golden combs in their long yellow hair. They were rocking themselves two together on the large dewdrops with which the leaves and the high grass were sprinkled. Sometimes the dewdrops would roll away, and then they fell down between the stems of the long grass, and caused a great deal of laughing and noise among the other little people. It was quite charming to watch them at play. Then they sang songs, and John remembered that he had learned those pretty songs when he was a little boy. Large speckled spiders, with silver crowns on their heads, were employed to spin suspension bridges and palaces from one hedge to another, and when the tiny drops fell upon them, they glittered in the moonlight like shining glass. This continued till sunrise. Then the little elves crept into the flower buds, and the wind seized the bridges and palaces, and fluttered them in the air like cobwebs.

As John left the wood, a strong man's voice called after him, " Hallo, comrade, where are you traveling? "

" Into the wide world," he replied; " I am only a poor lad; I have neither father nor mother, but God will help me."

" I am going into the wide world also," replied the Stranger; " shall we keep each other company? "

"With all my heart," said he; and so they went on together. Soon they began to like each other very much, for they were both good; but John found out that the Stranger was much more clever than himself. He had traveled all over the world, and could describe almost everything. The sun was high in the heavens when they seated themselves under a large tree to eat their breakfast, and at the same moment an old woman came toward them.

She was very old and almost bent double. She leaned upon a stick and carried on her back a bundle of firewood, which she had collected in the forest; her apron was tied round it, and John saw three great stems of fern and some

willow twigs peeping out. Just as she came close up to
them, her foot slipped and she fell to the ground screaming
loudly: poor old woman, she had broken her leg! John
proposed directly that they should carry the old woman
home to her cottage; but the Stranger opened his knapsack
and took out a box, in which he said he had a salve that
would quickly make her leg well and strong again, so that
she would be able to walk home herself, as if her leg had
never been broken. And all that he would ask in return was
the three fern stems which she carried in her apron.

"That is rather too high a price," said the old woman
nodding her head quite strangely. She did not seem at all
inclined to part with the fern stems. However, it was not
very agreeable to lie there with a broken leg, so she gave
them to him; and such was the power of the ointment, that
no sooner had he rubbed her leg with it than the old mother
rose up and walked even better than she had done before.
But then this wonderful ointment could not be bought at an
apothecary's.

"What can you want with those three fern rods?" asked
John of his fellow-traveler.

"O they will make capital brooms," said he; "and I like
them because I am a whimsical fellow." Then they walked
on together for a long distance.

"How dark the sky is becoming," said John; "and look
at those thick, heavy clouds."

"Those are not clouds," replied his fellow-traveler; "they
are mountains—large lofty mountains—on the tops of which
we should be above the clouds, in the pure, free air. Believe
me, it is delightful to ascend so high; tomorrow we shall be
there." But the mountains were not so near as they appeared;
they had to travel a whole day before they reached them,
and pass through black forests and piles of rock as large as
a town. The journey had been so fatiguing that John and
his fellow-traveler stopped to rest at a roadside inn, so that

they might gain strength for their journey on the morrow. In the large public room of the inn a great many persons were assembled to see a comedy performed by dolls. The showman had just erected his little theatre, and the people were sitting round the room to witness the performance. Right in front, in the very best place, sat a stout butcher, with a great bulldog by his side who seemed very much inclined to bite. He sat staring with all his eyes, and so indeed did every one else in the room. And then the play began. It was a pretty piece, with a king and queen in it, who sat on a beautiful throne, and had gold crowns on their heads. The trains to their dresses were very long, according to the fashion; while the prettiest of wooden dolls, with glass eyes and large moustaches, stood at the doors, and opened and shut them, that the fresh air might come into the room. It was a very pleasant play, not at all mournful; but just as the Queen stood up and walked across the stage, the great bulldog, who should have been held back by his master, made a spring forward, and caught the Queen in his teeth by the slender waist, so that it snapped in two. This was a very dreadful disaster. The poor man, who was exhibiting the dolls, was much annoyed, and quite sad about his Queen; she was the prettiest doll he had, and the bulldog had broken her head and shoulders off. But after all the people were gone away, the stranger, who came with John, said that he could soon set her to rights. And then he brought out his box and rubbed the doll with some of the salve with which he had cured the old woman when she broke her leg. As soon as this was done the doll's back became quite right again; her head and shoulders were fixed on, and she could even move her limbs herself: there was now no occasion to pull the wires, for the doll acted just like a living creature, excepting that she could not speak. The man to whom the show belonged was quite delighted at having a doll who could dance by herself without being pulled by the wires; none of the other dolls could do this.

During the night, when all the people at the inn were gone to bed, some one was heard to sigh so deeply and painfully, and the sighing continued for so long a time, that every one got up to see what could be the matter. The Showman went at once to his little theatre and found that it proceeded from the dolls, who all lay on the floor sighing piteously, and staring with their glass eyes; they all wanted to be rubbed with the ointment, so that, like the Queen, they might be able to move by themselves. The Queen threw herself on her kness, took off her beautiful crown, and, holding it in her hand, cried, "Take this from me, but do rub my husband and his courtiers."

The poor man who owned the theatre could scarcely refrain from weeping; he was so sorry that he could not help them. Then he immediately spoke to John's comrade, and promised him all the money he might receive at the next evening's performance, if he would only rub the ointment on four or five of his dolls. But the fellow-traveler said he did not require anything in return, excepting the sword which the Showman wore by his side. As soon as he received the sword he anointed six of the dolls with the ointment, and they were able immediately to dance so gracefully that all the living girls in the room could not help joining in the dance. The coachman danced with the cook, and the waiters with the chambermaids, and all the strangers joined; even the tongs and the fire shovel made an attempt, but they fell down after the first jump. So, after all, it was a very merry night. The next morning John and his companion left the inn to continue their journey through the great pine forests and over the high mountains. They arrived at last at such a great height that towns and villages lay beneath them, and the church steeples looked like little specks between the green trees. They could see for miles around, far away to places they had never visited, and John saw more of the beautiful world than he had ever known before. The sun shone brightly in the blue firmament above, and through the clear mountain air came the sound of the huntsman's horn, and the soft, sweet notes brought tears into his eyes, and he could not help exclaiming, "How good and loving God is to give us all this beauty and loveliness in the world to make us happy! "

His fellow-traveler stood by with folded hands, gazing on the dark woods and the towns bathed in the warm sunshine. At this moment there sounded over their heads sweet music. They looked up, and discovered a large white swan hovering in the air, and singing as never a bird sang before. But the song soon became weaker and weaker, the bird's head drooped, and he sunk slowly down, and lay dead at their feet.

"It is a beautiful bird," said the traveler, "and these large white wings are worth a great deal of money. I will take them with me. You see now that a sword will be very useful."

So he cut off the wings of the dead swan with one blow, and carried them away with him.

They now continued their journey over the mountains for many miles, till they at length reached a large city, containing hundreds of towers, that shone in the sunshine like silver. In the midst of the city stood a splendid marble palace, roofed with pure red gold, in which dwelt the King. John and his companion would not go into the town immediately; so they stopped at an inn outside the town, to change their clothes; for they wished to appear respectable as they walked through the streets. The landlord told them that the King was a very good man, who never injured any one; but as to his daughter, "Heaven defend us! "

She was indeed a wicked Princess. She possessed beauty enough—nobody could be more elegant or prettier than she was; but what of that? for she was a wicked witch; and in consequence of her conduct many noble young princes had

lost their lives. Any one was at liberty to make her an offer;
were he a prince or a beggar, it mattered not to her. She
would ask him to guess three things which she had just
thought of, and if he succeeded, he was to marry her, and
be king over all the land when her father died; but if he
could not guess these three things, then she ordered him
to be hanged or to have his head cut off. The old King, her
father, was very much grieved at her conduct, but he could
not prevent her from being so wicked, because he once said
he would have nothing more to do with her lovers; she
might do as she pleased. Each prince who came and tried
the three guesses, so that he might marry the Princess, had
been unable to find them out, and had been hanged or
beheaded. They had all been warned in time, and might
have left her alone, if they would. The old King became
at last so distressed at all these dreadful circumstances, that
for a whole day every year he and his soldiers knelt and
prayed that the Princess might become good; but she
continued as wicked as ever. The old women who drank
brandy would color it quite black before they drank it, to
show how they mourned; and what more could they do?

"What a horrible princess!" said John; "she ought to be
well flogged. If I were the old King, I would have her
punished in some way."

Just then they heard the people outside shouting, "Hurrah!" and, looking out, they saw the Princess passing by;
and she was really so beautiful that everybody forgot her
wickedness, and shouted, "Hurrah!" Twelve lovely maidens
in white silk dresses, holding golden tulips in their hands,
rode by her side on coal-black horses. The Princess herself
had a snow-white steed, decked with diamonds and rubies.
Her dress was of cloth of gold, and the whip she held in her
hand looked like a sunbeam. The golden crown on her head
glittered like the stars of heaven, and her mantle was formed

of thousands of butterflies' wings sewn together. Yet she herself was more beautiful than all.

When John saw her, his face became as red as a drop of blood, and he could scarcely utter a word. The Princess looked exactly like the beautiful lady with the golden crown, of whom he had dreamed on the night his father died. She appeared to him so lovely that he could not help loving her.

"It could not be true," he thought, "that she was really a wicked witch, who ordered people to be hanged or beheaded, if they could not guess her thoughts. Every one has permission to go and ask her hand, even the poorest beggar. I shall pay a visit to the palace," he said; "I must go, for I cannot help myself."

Then they all advised him not to attempt it; for he would be sure to share the same fate as the rest. His fellow-traveler also tried to persuade him against it; but John seemed quite sure of success. He brushed his shoes and his coat, washed his face and his hands, combed his soft flaxen hair, and then went out alone into the town, and walked to the palace.

"Come in," said the King, as John knocked at the door. John opened it, and the old King, in a dressing gown and embroidered slippers, came toward him. He had the crown on his head, carried his scepter in one hand, and the orb in the other. "Wait a bit," said he, and he placed the orb under his arm, so that he could offer the other hand to John; but when he found that John was another suitor, he began to weep so violently that both the scepter and the orb fell to the floor, and he was obliged to wipe his eyes with his dressing gown. Poor old King! "Let her alone," he said; "you will fare as badly as all the others. Come, I will show you." Then he led him out into the Princess' pleasure gardens, and there he saw a frightful sight. On every tree hung three or four king's sons who had wooed the Princess, but had not been able to guess the riddles she gave them. Their skeletons rattled in every breeze, so that the terrified birds never dared to venture into the garden. All the flowers were supported by human bones instead of sticks, and human skulls in the flowerpots grinned horribly. It was really a doleful garden for a princess. "Do you see all this?" said the old King; "your fate will be the same as those who are here, therefore do not attempt it. You really make me very unhappy—I take these things to heart so very much."

John kissed the good old King's hand, and said he was sure it would be all right, for he was quite enchanted with the beautiful Princess. Then the Princess herself came riding into the palace yard with all her ladies, and he wished her "Good morning." She looked wonderfully fair and lovely when she offered her hand to John, and he loved her more than ever. How could she be a wicked witch, as all the people asserted? He accompanied her into the hall, and the little pages offered them gingerbread nuts and sweetmeats; but the old King was so unhappy he could eat nothing, and besides, gingerbread nuts were too hard for him. It was decided that John should come to the palace the next day, when the judges and the whole of the counselors would be present, to try if he could guess the first riddle. If he succeeded, he would have to come a second time; but if not, he would lose his life—and no one had ever been able to guess even one. However, John was not at all anxious about the result of his trial; on the contrary, he was very merry. He thought only of the beautiful Princess, and believed that in some way he should have help, but how he knew not, and did not like to think about it; so he danced along the highroad as he went back to the inn, where he had left his fellow-traveler waiting for him. John could not refrain from telling him how gracious the Princess had been, and how beautiful she looked. He longed for the next day so much, that he might go to the palace and try his luck at guessing the riddles. But his comrade shook his head, and looked very mournful. "I do so wish you to do well," said he; "we might have continued together much longer, and now I am likely to lose you; you poor dear John! I could shed tears, but I will not make you unhappy on the last night we may be together. We will be merry, really merry this evening; tomorrow, after you are gone, I shall be able to weep undisturbed."

It was very quickly known among the inhabitants of the town that another suitor had arrived for the Princess, and there was great sorrow in consequence. The theatre remained closed, the women who sold sweetmeats tied crape round the sugar sticks, and the King and the priests were on their knees in the church. There was a great lamentation, for no one expected John to succeed better than those who had been suitors before.

In the evening John's comrade prepared a large bowl of punch, and said, "Now let us be merry, and drink to the health of the Princess." But after drinking two glasses, John became so sleepy, that he could not possibly keep his eyes open, and fell fast asleep. Then his fellow-traveler lifted him gently out of his chair, and laid him on the bed; and as soon as it was quite dark, he took the two large wings which he had cut from the dead swan, and tied them firmly to his own shoulders. Then he put into his pocket the largest of the three rods which he had obtained from the old woman who had fallen and broken her leg. After this he opened the window, and flew away over the town, straight towards the palace, and seated himself in a corner, under the window which looked into the bedroom of the Princess.

The town was perfectly still when the clocks struck a quarter to twelve. Presently the window opened, and the Princess, who had large black wings to her shoulders, and a long white mantle, flew away over the city towards a high mountain. The fellow-traveler, who had made himself invisible, so that she could not possibly see him, flew after her through the air, and whipped the Princess with his rod, so that the blood came whenever he struck her. Ah, it was a strange flight through the air! The wind caught her mantle, so that it spread out on all sides, like the large sail of a ship, and the moon shone through it. "How it hails, to be sure!" said the Princess, at each blow she received from the rod; and it served her right to be whipped.

At last she reached the side of the mountain, and knocked. The mountain opened with a noise like the roll of thunder, and the Princess went in. The traveler followed her; no one could see him, as he had made himself invisible. They went through a long, wide passage. A thousand gleaming spiders ran here and there on the walls, causing them to glitter as if they were illuminated with fire. They next entered a large hall built of silver and gold. Large red and blue flowers shone on the walls, looking like sunflowers in size; but no one could dare to pluck them, for the stems were hideous poisonous snakes, and the flowers were flames of fire, darting out of their jaws. Shining glowworms covered the ceiling, and sky-blue bats flapped their transparent wings. Altogether the place had a frightful appearance. In the middle of the floor stood a throne supported by four skeleton horses, whose harness had been made by fiery-red spiders. The throne itself was made of milk-white glass, and the cushions were little black mice, each biting the other's tail. Over it hung a canopy of rose-colored spider webs, spotted with the prettiest little green flies, which sparkled like precious stones. On the throne sat an old Magician with a crown on his ugly head, and a scepter in his hand. He kissed the Princess on the forehead, seated her by his side on the splendid throne, and then the music commenced. Great black grasshoppers played the mouth organ, and the owl struck herself on the body instead of a drum. It was altogether a ridiculous concert. Little black goblins with false lights in their caps danced about the hall; but no one could see the traveler, and he had placed himself just behind the throne where he could see and hear everything. The courtiers who came in afterwards looked noble and grand; but any one with common sense could see what they really were, only broomsticks, with cabbages for heads. The Magician had given them life, and dressed them in embroidered robes. It answered very well, as they were only wanted for show. After there had been a little dancing, the Princess told the Magician that she had a new suitor, and asked him what she should think of for the suitor to guess when he came to the castle the next morning.

"Listen to what I say," said the Magician; "you must choose something very easy: he is less likely to guess it then. Think of one of your shoes: he will never imagine it is that. Then cut his head off; and mind you do not forget to bring his eyes with you tomorrow night, that I may eat them."

The Princess curtesied low, and said she would not forget the eyes.

The Magician then opened the mountain and she flew home again, but the traveler followed and flogged her so much with the rod, that she sighed quite deeply about the heavy hailstorm, and made as much haste as she could to get back to her bedroom through the window. The traveler then returned to the inn where John still slept, took off his wings and lay down on the bed, for he was very tired. Early in the morning John awoke, and when his fellow-traveler got up, he said that he had had a very wonderful dream about the Princess and her shoe; he therefore advised John to ask her if she had not thought of her shoe. Of course the traveler knew this from what the Magician in the mountain had said.

"I may as well say that as anything else," said John. "Perhaps your dream may come true; still I will say farewell, for if I guess wrong I shall never see you again."

Then they embraced each other, and John went into the town and walked to the palace. The great hall was full of people, and the judges sat in armchairs, with eider-down

cushions to rest their heads upon, because they had so much
to think of. The old King stood near, wiping his eyes with
his white handkerchief. When the Princess entered, she
looked even more beautiful than she had appeared the day
before, and greeted every one present most gracefully; but
to John she gave her hand, and said, "Good morning to you."

Now came the time for John to guess what she was
thinking of; and O, how kindly she looked at him as she
spoke. But when he uttered the single word *shoe*, she turned
as pale as a ghost; all her wisdom could not help her, for
he had guessed rightly. O, how pleased the old King was!
It was quite amusing to see how he capered about. All the
people clapped their hands, both on his account and John's,
who had guessed rightly the first time. His fellow-traveler
was glad also, when he heard how successful John had been.
But John folded his hands, and thanked God, who, he felt
quite sure, would help him again; and he knew he had to
guess twice more. The evening passed pleasantly like the
one preceding. While John slept, his companion flew behind
the Princess to the mountain, and flogged her even harder
than before; this time he had taken two rods with him.
No one saw him go in with her, and he heard all that was
said. The Princess this time was to think of a glove, and he
told John as if he had again heard it in a dream. The next
day, therefore, he was able to guess correctly the second
time, and it caused great rejoicing at the palace. The whole
court jumped about as they had seen the King do the day
before, but the Princess lay on the sofa, and would not say
a single word. All now depended upon John. If he only
guessed rightly the third time, he would marry the Princess,
and reign over the kingdom after the death of the old King;
but if he failed, he would lose his life, and the Magician
would have his beautiful blue eyes. That evening John said
his prayers and went to bed very early, and soon fell asleep
calmly. But his companion tied on his wings to his shoulders,

took three rods, and, with his sword at his side, flew to the palace. It was a very dark night, and so stormy that the tiles flew from the roofs of the houses, and the trees in the garden upon which the skeletons hung bent themselves like reeds before the wind. The lightning flashed, and the thunder rolled in one long-continued peal all night. The window of the castle opened, and the Princess flew out. She was pale as death, but she laughed at the storm as if it were not bad enough. Her white mantle fluttered in the wind like a large sail, and the traveler flogged her with the three rods till the blood trickled down, and at last she could scarcely fly; she contrived, however, to reach the mountain. "What a hailstorm!" she said, as she entered; "I have never been out in such weather as this."

"Yes, there may be too much of a good thing sometimes," said the Magician.

Then the Princess told him that John had guessed rightly the second time, and if he succeeded the next morning, he would win, and she could never come to the mountain again, or practice magic as she had done, and therefore she was quite unhappy.

"I will find out something for you to think of which he will never guess, unless he is a greater conjuror than myself," said the Magician. "But now let us be merry."

Then he took the Princess by both hands, and they danced with all the little goblins and jack-o'-lanterns in the room. The red spiders sprang here and there on the walls quite as merrily, and the flowers of fire appeared as if they were throwing out sparks. The owl beat the drum, the crickets whistled, and the grasshoppers played the mouth organ. It was a very ridiculous ball. After they had danced enough, the Princess was obliged to go home, for fear she should be missed at the palace. The Magician offered to go with her, that they might be company to each other on the way. Then they flew away through the bad weather, and the

traveler followed them, and broke his three rods across their
shoulders. The Magician had never been out in such a
hailstorm as this. Just by the palace the Magician stopped
to wish the Princess farewell, and to whisper in her ear,
" Tomorrow think of my head."

But the traveler heard it, and just as the Princess slipped
through the window into her bedroom, and the Magician
turned round to fly back to the mountain, he seized him by
the long black beard, and with his saber cut off the wicked
conjuror's head just behind his shoulders, so that he could
not even see who it was. He threw the body into the sea
to the fishes, and, after dipping the head into the water, he
tied it up in a silk handkerchief, took it with him to the inn,
and then went to bed. The next morning he gave John the
handkerchief, and told him not to untie it till the Princess
asked him what she was thinking of. There were so many
people in the great hall of the palace that they stood as
thick as radishes tied together in a bundle. The council sat
in their armchairs with the white cushions. The old King
wore new robes, and the golden crown and scepter had been
polished up so that he looked quite smart. But the Princess
was very pale, and wore a black dress as if she were going
to a funeral.

" What have I thought of? " asked the Princess, of John.
He immediately untied the handkerchief, and was himself
quite frightened when he saw the head of the ugly Magician.
Every one shuddered, for it was terrible to look at; but
the Princess sat like a statue and could not utter a single
word. At length she rose and gave John her hand, for he had
guessed rightly.

She looked at no one, but sighed deeply, and said, " You
are my master now; this evening our marriage must take
place."

" I am very much pleased to hear it," said the old King.
" It is just what I wish."

Then all the people shouted "Hurrah!" The band played music in the street, the bells rang, and the cake-women took the black crape off the sugar sticks. There was universal joy. Three oxen, stuffed with ducks and chickens, were roasted whole in the market place, where every one might help himself to a slice. The fountains spouted forth the most delicious wine, and whoever bought a penny loaf at the baker's received six large buns, full of raisins, as a present. In the evening the whole town was illuminated. The soldiers fired off cannons, and the boys let off crackers. There was eating and drinking, dancing and jumping everywhere. In the palace, the high-born gentlemen and the beautiful ladies danced with each other, and they could be heard at a great distance singing the following song—

> *Here are maidens, young and fair,*
> *Dancing in the summer air;*
> *Like to spinning wheels at play,*
> *Pretty maidens dance away—*
> *Dance the spring and summer through*
> *Till the sole falls from your shoe.*

But the Princess was still a witch, and she could not love John. His fellow-traveler had thought of that, so he gave John three feathers out of the swan's wings, and a little bottle with a few drops in it. He told him to place a large bath full of water by the Princess's bed, and put the feathers and the drops into it. Then, at the moment she was about to get into bed, he must give her a little push, so that she might fall into the water, and then dip her three times. This would destroy the power of the Magician, and she would love him very much.

John did all that his companion told him to do. The Princess shrieked aloud when he dipped her under the water the first time, and struggled under his hands in the form of a great black swan with fiery eyes. As she rose the second time

from the water, the swan had become white, with a black
ring round its neck. John allowed the water to close once
more over the bird, and at the same time it changed into a
most beautiful Princess. She was more lovely even than
before, and thanked him, while her eyes sparkled with tears,
for having broken the spell of the Magician.

The next day, the King came with the whole court to
offer their congratulations, and stayed till quite late. Last of
all came the traveling companion; he had his staff in his
hand and his knapsack on his back. John kissed him many
times and told him he must not go, he must remain with
him, for he was the cause of all his good fortune. But the
traveler shook his head, and said gently and kindly, "No:
my time is up now; I have only paid my debt to you. Do
you remember the dead man whom the bad people wished
to throw out of his coffin? You gave all you possessed that
he might rest in his grave; I am the dead man." As he said
this, he vanished.

The wedding festivities lasted a whole month. John and
his Princess loved each other dearly, and the old King lived
to see many a happy day, when he took their little children
on his knees and let them play with his scepter. And John
became king over the whole country.

Little Ida's Flowers

"My poor flowers are dead," said little Ida. "They were so pretty yesterday evening, and now all the leaves are hanging down quite withered. Why do they do that?" she asked of the student who sat on the sofa. She liked him very much; he could tell the most amusing stories and cut out the prettiest pictures—hearts, and ladies dancing, castles with doors that opened, as well as flowers. He was a delightful student. "Why do the flowers look so faded today?" she asked again, and pointed to her nosegay, which was quite withered.

"Don't you know what is the matter with them?" said the student. "The flowers were at a ball last night, and it is no wonder they hang their heads."

"But flowers cannot dance?" cried little Ida.

"Yes, indeed, they can," replied the student. "When it grows dark, and everybody is asleep, they jump about quite merrily. They have a ball almost every night."

"Can children go to these balls?"

"Yes," said the student, "little daisies and lilies of the valley."

"Where do the flowers dance?" asked little Ida.

"Have you not often seen the large castle outside the gates of the town, where the king lives in summer and where the beautiful garden is full of flowers? And have you not fed the swans with bread when they swam towards you in the lake? Well, the flowers have capital balls there, believe me."

"I was in the garden yesterday with my mother," said Ida. "But all the leaves were off the trees and there was not a single flower left. Where are they? I used to see so many in the summer."

"They are in the castle," replied the student. "You must know that as soon as the king and all the court are gone into the town, the flowers run out of the garden into the castle, and you should see how merry they are. The two most beautiful roses seat themselves on the throne, and are called the king and queen. Then all the red cockscombs range themselves on each side and bow. These are the lords-in-waiting. After that the pretty flowers come in and there is a grand ball. The blue violets represent little naval cadets and dance with hyacinths and crocuses, which they call young ladies. The tulips and tiger lilies are the old ladies who sit and watch the dancing, so that everything may be conducted with order and propriety."

"But," said little Ida, "is there no one there to hurt the flowers for dancing in the king's castle?"

"No one knows anything about it," said the student. "The old steward of the castle, who has to watch there at night, sometimes comes in. He carries a great bunch of keys, and as soon as the flowers hear the keys rattle, they run and hide themselves behind the long curtains and stand quite still, just peeping their heads out. Then the steward says, 'I smell flowers here,' but he cannot see them."

"Oh, how capital!" said little Ida, clapping her hands. "Should I be able to see these flowers?"

"Yes," said the student. "Mind you think of it next time you go out. No doubt you will see them if you peep through the window. I did so today, and I saw a long yellow lily lying stretched out on the sofa. She was a court lady."

" Can the flowers from the Botanical Gardens go to these balls? " asked Ida. "It is such a distance! "

" Oh, yes," said the student, "whenever they like, for they can fly. Have you not seen those beautiful red, white, and yellow butterflies that look like flowers? They were flowers once. They have flown off their stalks into the air, and flap their leaves as if they were little wings to make them fly. Then, if they behave well, they obtain permission to fly about during the day, instead of being obliged to sit still on their stems at home. And so in time their leaves become real wings. It may be, however, that the flowers in the Botanical Gardens have never been to the king's palace, and, therefore, they know nothing of the merry doings which take place there at night. I will tell you what to do, and the botanical professor, who lives close by here, will be so surprised. You know him very well, do you not? Well, next time you go into his garden, you must tell one of the flowers that there is going to be a grand ball at the castle. Then that flower will tell all the others and they will fly away to the castle as soon as possible. And when the professor walks into his garden, there will not be a single flower left. How he will wonder what has become of them! "

" But how can one flower tell another? Flowers cannot speak."

" No, certainly not," replied the student, "but they can make signs. Have you not often seen that when the wind blows they nod at one another and rustle all their green leaves? "

" Can the professor understand the signs? " asked Ida.

" Yes, to be sure he can. He went one morning into his garden and saw a stinging nettle making signs with its leaves to a beautiful red carnation. It was saying, 'You are so pretty, I like you very much.' But the professor did not approve of such nonsense, so he clapped his hands on the nettle to stop it. Then the leaves, which are its fingers, stung him so sharply that he has never ventured to touch a nettle since."

"Oh, how funny!" said Ida, and she laughed.

"How can anyone put such notions into a child's head?" said a tiresome lawyer, who had come to pay a visit. He did not like the student, and would grumble when he saw him cutting out droll or amusing pictures. Sometimes it would be a man hanging on a gibbet and holding a heart in his hand as if he had been stealing hearts. Sometimes it was an old witch riding through the air on a broom and carrying her husband on her nose. But the lawyer did not like such jokes, and he would say as he had just said, "How can anyone put such nonsense into a child's head? What absurd fancies they are!"

But to little Ida, all these stories which the student told her about the flowers seemed very droll, and she thought over them a great deal. The flowers did hang their heads, because they had been dancing all night and were very tired, and most likely they were ill. Then she took them into the room where a number of toys lay on a pretty little table, and the whole of the table drawer besides was full of beautiful things. Her doll Sophy lay in the doll's bed asleep, and little Ida said to her, "You must really get up, Sophy, and be content to lie in the drawer tonight. The poor flowers are ill, and they must lie in your bed. Then perhaps they will get well again." So she took out the doll, who looked quite cross and said not a single word, for she was angry at being turned out of her bed. Ida placed the flowers in the doll's bed and drew the quilt over them. Then she told them to lie quite still and be good while she made some tea for them, so that they might be quite well and able to get up the next morning. And she drew the curtains close round the little bed, so that the sun might not shine in their eyes. During the whole evening she could not help thinking of what the student had told her. And before she

went to bed herself, she peeped behind the curtains into
the garden where all her mother's beautiful flowers grew—
hyacinths and tulips, and many others. Then she whispered
to them quite softly, "I know you are going to a ball
tonight." But the flowers appeared as if they did not
understand, and not a leaf moved; still Ida felt quite sure
she knew all about it.

She lay awake a long time after she was in bed, thinking
how pretty it must be to see all the beautiful flowers
dancing in the king's garden. "I wonder if my flowers have
really been there?" she said to herself, and then she fell
asleep. In the night she awoke; she had been dreaming of
the flowers and of the student, as well as of the tiresome
lawyer who found fault with him. It was quite still in Ida's
bedroom; the night lamp burned on the table and her father
and mother were asleep. "I wonder if my flowers are still
lying in Sophy's bed?" she thought to herself. "How much
I should like to know!" She raised herself a little and
glanced at the door of the room where all her flowers and
playthings lay. It was partly open, and as she listened, it
seemed as if someone in the room was playing the piano, but
softly and more prettily than she had ever before heard it.
"Now all the flowers are certainly dancing in there," she
thought. "Oh, how much I should like to see them!" But
she did not dare to move for fear of disturbing her father
and mother. "If they would only come in here," she thought,
but they did not come. And the music continued to play
so beautifully, and was so pretty, that she could resist no
longer. She crept out of her little bed, went softly to the
door, and looked into the room.

Oh, what a splendid sight there was to be sure! There
was no night lamp burning, but the room appeared quite
light, for the moon shone through the window upon the
floor, and made it almost like day. All the hyacinths and
tulips stood in two long rows down the room. Not a single

flower remained in the window, and the flowerpots were all empty. The flowers were dancing gracefully on the floor, making turns and holding each other by their long green leaves as they swung round. At the piano sat a large yellow lily which little Ida was sure she had seen in the summer, for she remembered the student saying she was very much like Miss Lina, one of Ida's friends. They all laughed at him then, but now it seemed to little Ida as if the tall yellow flower was really like the young lady. She had just the same manners while playing, bending her long yellow face from side to side, and nodding in time to the beautiful music.

Then she saw a large purple crocus jump into the middle of the table where the playthings stood, go up to the doll's bedstead and draw back the curtains. There lay the sick flowers, but they got up directly and nodded to the others as a sign that they wished to dance with them. The old rough doll with the broken mouth stood up and bowed to the pretty flowers. They did not look ill at all now, but jumped about and were very merry. Yet none of them noticed little Ida. Presently it seemed as if something fell from the table. Ida looked that way and saw a slight carnival rod jumping down among the flowers as if it belonged to them. It was, however, very smooth and neat, and a little wax doll with a broad-brimmed hat on her head, like the one worn by the lawyer, sat upon it. The carnival rod hopped about among the flowers on its three red stilted feet, and stamped quite loud when it danced the mazurka. The flowers could not do this dance—they were too light to stamp in that manner.

All at once the wax doll on the carnival rod seemed to grow larger and taller, and it turned around and said to the flowers, " How can you put such things in a child's head? They are all foolish fancies." And then the doll was exactly like the lawyer with the broad-brimmed hat, and looked as yellow and as cross as he did. But the rough doll struck

him on his thin legs, and he shrunk up again and became
quite a little wax doll. This was very amusing, and Ida could
not help laughing. The carnival rod went on dancing, and
the lawyer was obliged to dance also. It made no difference
whether he made himself great and tall, or remained a little
wax doll with a large black hat; still he must dance. At last
some of the flowers interceded for him, especially those
who had lain in the doll's bed, and the carnival rod gave
up his dancing. At that moment a loud knocking was heard
in the drawer, where Ida's doll Sophy lay with many other
toys. Then the rough doll ran to the end of the table, laid
himself flat down upon it, and began to pull the drawer
out a little way.

Sophy raised herself and looked round quite astonished.
"There must be a ball here tonight," she said. "Why did
not somebody tell me? "

"Will you dance with me? " said the rough doll.

"You are the right sort to dance with, certainly," said she,
turning her back upon him.

Then she seated herself on the edge of the drawer and
thought that perhaps one of the flowers would ask her to
dance, but none of them did. Then she coughed, "Hem, hem,
a-hem "—but for all that no partner came. The shabby doll
now danced quite alone, and not very badly, after all. As
none of the flowers seemed to notice Sophy, she let herself
down from the drawer to the floor, so as to make a very
great noise. All the flowers came round her directly and
asked if she had hurt herself, especially those who had lain
in her bed. But she was not hurt at all, and Ida's flowers
thanked her for the use of the nice bed and were very kind
to her. They led her into the middle of the room, where the
moon shone, and danced with her, while all the other
flowers formed a circle round them. Then Sophy was very
happy and said they might keep her bed: she did not mind
lying in the drawer at all. But the flowers thanked her very

much and said, "We cannot live long. Tomorrow morning we shall be dead, and you must tell little Ida to bury us in the garden, near the grave of the canary. In the summer we shall wake up again and be more beautiful than ever."

"No, you must not die," said Sophy, as she kissed the flowers.

Then the door of the room opened and a number of beautiful flowers danced in. Ida could not imagine where they could have come from, unless they were the flowers from the king's garden. First came two lovely roses with little golden crowns on their heads. These were the king and queen. Beautiful stocks and carnations followed, bowing to everyone present. They also had music with them. Large poppies and peonies had pea shells for instruments, and blew into them till they were quite red in the face. The bunches of blue hyacinths and the little white snowdrops jingled their bell-like flowers, as if they were real bells. Then came many more flowers: blue violets, purple heart's-ease, daisies, and lilies of the valley, and they all danced together, and kissed each other. It was very beautiful to behold.

At last the flowers wished each other good night. Then little Ida crept back into bed again, and dreamt of all she had seen. When she arose the next morning, she went quickly to the little table to see if the flowers were still there. She drew aside the curtains of the little bed. There they all lay, but quite faded; much more so than the day before. Sophy was lying in the drawer where Ida had placed her, but she looked very sleepy.

"Do you remember what the flowers told you to say to me?" asked little Ida. But Sophy looked quite stupid and said not a single word.

"You are not kind at all," said Ida. "And yet they all danced with you."

Then she took a little paper box on which were painted beautiful birds, and laid the dead flowers in it.

"This shall be your pretty coffin," she said. "And by and by, when my cousins come to visit me, they shall help me to bury you out in the garden, so that next summer you may grow up again more beautiful than ever."

Her cousins were two good-tempered boys whose names were James and Adolphus. Their father had given them each a bow and arrow, and they had brought them to show Ida. She told them about the poor flowers which were dead, and as soon as they obtained permission they went with her to bury them. The two boys walked first with their crossbows on their shoulders, and little Ida followed, carrying the pretty box containing the dead flowers. They dug a little grave in the garden. Ida kissed her flowers, and then laid them, with the box, in the earth. James and Adolphus then fired their crossbows over the grave, as they had neither guns nor cannons.

Thumbelina

There was once a woman who wished very much to have a child, but she could not obtain her wish. At last she went to a fairy and said, "I should so very much like to have a little child. Can you tell me where I can find one?"

"Oh, that can be easily managed," said the fairy. "Here is a grain of barley different from the kind that grows in the fields and that the chickens eat. Plant it in a flowerpot and see what will happen."

"Thank you," said the woman and gave the fairy twelve pennies, which was the price of the barleycorn. Then she went home and planted it. Immediately there grew up a large handsome flower, something like a tulip in appearance, but with leaves tightly closed as if it were still a bud.

"It is a beautiful flower," said the woman, and she kissed the red and golden colored leaves. While she did so the flower opened and she could see that it was a real tulip. Within the flower, upon the green velvet stamens, sat a very delicate and graceful little maiden. She was scarcely half as long as a thumb, and they gave her the name of Little Thumb, or Thumbelina, because she was so small. A walnut shell, elegantly polished, served her for a cradle. Her bed was formed of blue violet leaves, with a rose leaf for a counterpane. Here she slept at night, but during the day she amused herself on a table, where the woman placed a plate full of water. Round this plate were flowers with their stems in the water, and upon it floated a large tulip petal which served Thumbelina for a boat. Here the little maiden sat and rowed from side to side, with two oars made of white horsehair. It really was a very pretty sight. Thumbelina could sing so softly and sweetly that nothing like her singing had ever before been heard.

One night as she lay in her pretty bed, a large, ugly, wet toad crept through a broken pane of glass in the window, and leaped right upon the table where Thumbelina lay sleeping under her rose leaf quilt. "What a pretty little wife she would make for my son!" said the toad, and she took up the walnut shell in which little Thumbelina lay asleep, and jumped through the window with it into the garden.

In the swampy margin of a broad stream in the garden lived the toad with her son. He was uglier even than his mother! When he saw the pretty little maiden in her elegant bed, he could only cry, "Croak, croak, croak."

"Don't speak so loud or she will awake," said the old toad. "And then she might run away, for she is as light as swan's down. We will place her on one of the water lily leaves out in the stream. It will be like an island to her—she is so light and small—and then she cannot escape. And while she is away we will make haste and prepare the state-room under the marsh, in which you are to live when you are married."

Far out in the stream grew a number of water lilies with broad green leaves, which seemed to float on the top of the water. The largest of these leaves appeared farther off than the rest, and the old toad swam out to it with the walnut shell, in which little Thumbelina lay still asleep. The little creature woke very early in the morning, and began to cry bitterly when she found where she was. She could see nothing but water on every side of the large green leaf and no way of reaching the land. Meanwhile the old toad

was very busy under the marsh, decking her room with
rushes and wild yellow flowers, to make it look pretty for
her new daughter-in-law. Then she swam out with her
ugly son to the leaf on which she had placed poor little
Thumbelina. She wanted to fetch the pretty bed, that she
might put it in the bridal chamber to be ready for her.

The old toad bowed low to her in the water and said,
"Here is my son. He will be your husband and you will
live happily together in the marsh by the stream."

"Croak, croak, croak," was all her son could say for
himself. So the toads took up the elegant little bed and
swam away with it, leaving Thumbelina all alone on the
green leaf, where she sat and wept. She could not bear to
think of living with the old toad and having her ugly son for
a husband. The little fishes who swam about in the water
beneath her had seen the toad and had heard what she said,
so they lifted their heads above the water to look at the
little maiden. As soon as they caught sight of her they saw
she was very pretty, and it made them sorry to think that
she must go and live with the ugly toads. "No, that must
never be!" So they assembled together in the water around
the green stalk which held the leaf on which the little maiden
stood, and gnawed it away at the root with their teeth.
Then the leaf floated down the stream, carrying Thumbelina
far away, out of reach of land.

She sailed past many towns, and the little birds in the
bushes saw her and sang, "What a lovely little creature!"
The leaf swam with her farther and farther till it brought
her to other lands. A graceful white butterfly constantly
fluttered round her, and at last alighted on the leaf. Thumbelina pleased him, and she was glad of it for now the
toad could not possibly reach her, and the country through
which she sailed was beautiful, and the sun shone upon
the water till it glittered like liquid gold. She took off her
sash and tied one end of it round the butterfly and fastened

the other end to the leaf, which now glided on much faster than ever, taking little Thumbelina with it. Presently a large cockchafer flew by. The moment he caught sight of her, he seized her round her delicate waist with his claws and flew with her into a tree. The green leaf floated away on the brook, and the butterfly flew with it, for he was fastened to it and could not get away.

Oh, how frightened little Thumbelina felt when the cockchafer flew with her to the tree! But especially was she sorry for the beautiful white butterfly which she had fastened to the leaf, for if he could not free himself he would die of hunger. But the cockchafer did not trouble himself at all about the matter. He seated himself by her side on a large green leaf, gave her some honey from the flowers to eat, and told her she was very pretty, though not in the least like a cockchafer. After a time, all the cockchafers who lived in the tree came to visit her. They stared, and then the young lady cockchafers turned up their feelers and said, " She has only two legs. How ugly that looks! "

" She has no feelers," said another.

" Her waist is quite slim. She is just like a human being. Oh, she is ugly! " said all the lady cockchafers, although Thumbelina was very pretty.

The cockchafer who had run away with her believed all the others when they said she was ugly, and would have nothing more to do with her, and told her she might go where she liked. Then he flew down with her from the tree and placed her on a daisy, and she wept at the thought that she was so ugly that even the cockchafers would have nothing to say to her. And all the while she was really the loveliest creature that one could imagine, and as tender and delicate as a beautiful roseleaf.

During the whole summer poor little Thumbelina lived quite alone in the wide forest. She wove herself a bed with blades of grass, and hung it up under a broad leaf to protect herself from the rain. She sucked the honey from the flowers for food, and drank the dew from their leaves every morning. So passed away the summer and the autumn, and then came the winter—the long, cold winter. All the birds who had sung to her so sweetly had flown away, and the trees and the flowers had withered. The large clover leaf under which she had lived was now rolled together and shriveled up; nothing remained of it but a yellow withered stalk. She felt dreadfully cold, for her clothes were torn and she was herself so frail and delicate that poor Thumbelina was nearly frozen to death. It began to snow too, and the snowflakes, as they fell upon her, were like a whole shovelful falling upon one of us, for we are tall while she was only an inch high. Then she wrapped herself up in a dry leaf, but it cracked in the middle and could not keep her warm, and she shivered with cold.

Near the wood in which she had been living lay a large grain field, but the grain had been cut a long time. Nothing remained but the bare dry stubble standing up out of the frozen ground. It was to her like struggling through a large wood. Oh, how she shivered with the cold! She came at last to the door of a field mouse, who had a little den under the stubble. There dwelt the field mouse in warmth and comfort, with a whole roomful of grain, a kitchen, and a beautiful dining room. Poor little Thumbelina stood before the door just like a little beggar girl, and begged for a handful of barley, for she had been without a morsel to eat for two days.

"You poor little creature," said the field mouse, who was really a good old field mouse. "Come into my warm room and dine with me." She was so pleased with Thumbelina that she said, "You are quite welcome to stay with me all winter, if you like. But you must keep my rooms clean and neat, and tell me stories, for I like to hear them very much."

And Thumbelina did all the field mouse asked her, and found herself very comfortable.

"We shall have a visitor soon," said the field mouse one day. "My neighbor pays me a visit once a week. He is even better off than I am. He has rooms, and wears a beautiful black velvet coat. If you could only have him for a husband, you would be well provided for indeed. But he is blind; so you must tell him some of your prettiest stories."

Thumbelina did not feel at all interested about this neighbor, for he was a mole. However, he came and paid his visit, dressed in his black velvet coat.

"He is very rich and learned, and his house is twenty times larger than mine," said the field mouse.

He was rich and learned, no doubt, but he always spoke slightingly of the sun and the pretty flowers, because he had never seen them. Thumbelina was obliged to sing to him, "Ladybird, ladybird, fly away home," and many other pretty songs. And the mole fell in love with her because she had such a sweet voice, but he said nothing yet, for he was very cautious. A short time before, the mole had dug a long passage under the earth, which led from the dwelling of the field mouse to his own, and here she had permission to walk with Thumbelina whenever she liked. But he warned them not to be alarmed at the sight of a dead bird which lay in the passage. It was a perfect bird, with a beak and feathers, and could not have been dead long, and was lying just where the mole had made his passage.

The mole took a piece of phosphorescent wood in his mouth, and it glittered like fire in the dark. Then he went before them to light them through the long, dark passage. When they came to the spot where lay the dead bird, the mole pushed his broad nose through the ceiling, the earth gave way so that there was a large hole, and the daylight shone into the passage. In the middle of the floor lay a dead swallow, his beautiful wings folded close to his sides, his

feet and his head drawn up under his feathers. The poor
bird had evidently died of the cold. It made little Thumbelina very sad to see it, for she greatly loved the little birds
who had sung and twittered for her so beautifully all the
summer. But the mole pushed it aside with his crooked legs
and said, "He will sing no more now. How miserable it must
be to be born a little bird. I am thankful that none of my
children will ever be birds, who can do nothing but cry,
'Tweet, tweet,' and always die of hunger in the winter."

"Yes, you may well say that, you clever mole," exclaimed
the field mouse. "What is the use of his twittering, for when
winter comes he must either starve or be frozen to death?
Still birds are very highbred, I suppose."

Thumbelina said nothing, but when the two others had
turned their backs on the bird, she stooped down and stroked
aside the soft feathers which covered the head, and kissed
the closed eyelids. "Perhaps this was the one who sang to
me so sweetly in the summer," she said. "And how much
pleasure you gave me, you dear pretty bird."

The mole now stopped up the hole through which the
daylight shone, and then accompanied the ladies home. But
during the night, as Thumbelina could not sleep, she got out
of bed and wove a large beautiful carpet of hay. Then she
carried it to the dead bird and spread it over him, with some
down from the flowers which she had found in the field
mouse's room. It was as soft as wool, and she spread some
of it on each side of the bird so that he might lie warmly
in the cold earth. "Farewell, you pretty little bird," said
she. "Farewell. Thank you for your delightful singing during
the summer, when all the trees were green and the warm
sun shone upon us." Then she laid her head on the bird's
breast, and she was alarmed immediately, for it seemed as
if something inside the bird went thump, thump. It was the
bird's heart. He was not really dead—only benumbed with
the cold—and the warmth had restored him to life.

In autumn, all the swallows fly away into warm countries,
but if one happens to linger and the cold seizes it, it
becomes frozen and falls down as if dead. It remains where
it fell, and the cold snow covers it. Thumbelina trembled
very much: she was quite frightened, for the bird was large,
a great deal larger than herself—she was only an inch high.
But she took courage, laid the wool more thickly over the
poor swallow, and then brought a leaf which she had used
for her own counterpane and laid it over the head of the
poor bird. The next night she again stole out to see him.
He was alive but very weak. He could only open his eyes
for a moment to look at Thumbelina, who stood holding a
piece of decayed wood in her hand, for she had no other
lantern.

"Thank you, pretty little maiden," said the sick swallow.
"I have been so nicely warmed that I shall soon regain my
strength and be able to fly about in the warm sunshine."

"Oh," said she, "it is cold out of doors now. It is snowing
and freezing. Stay in your warm bed. I will take care of you."

Then she brought the swallow some water in a flower leaf.
And after he had drunk, he told her that he had wounded
one of his wings in a thornbush and could not fly as fast
as the others, who were soon far away on their journey to
warm countries. Then at last he had fallen to the earth and
could remember no more. He did not know how he came
to where she had found him. The whole winter the swallow
remained underground, and Thumbelina nursed him with
care and love. Neither the mole nor the field mouse knew
anything about it, for they did not like swallows.

Very soon the springtime came and the sun warmed the
earth. Then the swallow bade farewell to Thumbelina, and
she opened the hole in the ceiling which the mole had made.
The sun shone in upon them so beautifully that the swallow
asked her if she would go with him. She could sit on his
back, he said, and he would fly away with her into the green

woods. But Thumbelina knew it would make the field mouse feel very sad if she left her in that manner and said, "No, I cannot."

"Farewell, then. Farewell, you good, pretty little maiden," said the swallow and flew out into the sunshine.

Thumbelina looked after him, and the tears rose in her eyes. She was very fond of the poor swallow.

"Tweet, tweet," sang the bird as he flew out into the green woods, and Thumbelina felt very sad. She was not allowed to go out into the warm sunshine. The corn which had been sown in the field over the house of the field mouse had grown up high into the air, and formed a thick wood to Thumbelina, who was only an inch in height.

"You are going to be married, Thumbelina," said the field mouse. "My neighbor has asked for you. What good fortune for a poor child like you! Now we will prepare your wedding clothes. They must be both woolen and linen. Nothing must be wanting when you are the mole's wife."

Thumbelina had to turn the spindle, and the field mouse hired four spiders who were to weave day and night. Every evening the mole visited her and was continually speaking of the time when the summer would be over. Then he would keep his wedding day with Thumbelina, but now the heat of the sun was so great that it burned the earth and made it quite hard, like a stone. As soon as the summer was over, the wedding should take place, but Thumbelina was not at all pleased, for she did not like the tiresome mole. Every morning when the sun rose, and every evening when it went down, she would creep out at the door. And as the wind blew aside the leaves of the corn so that she could see the blue sky, she thought how beautiful and bright it seemed out there, and wished so much to see her dear swallow again. But he never returned. By this time he had flown far away into the lovely green forest.

When autumn arrived, Thumbelina had her outfit quite

ready, and the field mouse said to her, "In four weeks the wedding must take place."

Then Thumbelina wept, and said she would not marry the disagreeable mole.

"Nonsense," replied the field mouse. "Now don't be obstinate, or I shall bite you with my teeth. He is a very handsome mole. The queen herself does not wear more beautiful velvets and furs. His kitchens and cellars are quite full. You ought to be thankful for such good fortune."

So the wedding day was fixed, on which the mole was to fetch Thumbelina away to live with him deep under the earth, and never again to see the warm sun, because *he* did not like it. The poor child was very unhappy at the thought of saying farewell to the beautiful sun, and as the field mouse had given her permission to stand at the door, she went to look at it once more.

"Farewell, bright sun," she cried, stretching out her arm towards it. And then she walked a short distance from the house. The corn had been cut, and only the dry stubble remained in the fields. "Farewell, farewell," she repeated, twining her arm round a little red flower that grew just by her side. "Greet the little swallow for me, if you should see him again."

"Tweet, tweet," sounded over her head suddenly. She looked up, and there was the swallow himself flying close by. As soon as he spied Thumbelina, he was delighted. And then she told him how unwilling she felt to marry the ugly mole, and to live always beneath the earth and never see the bright sun any more. And as she told him she wept.

"Cold winter is coming," said the swallow, "and I am going to fly away into warmer countries. Will you go with me? You can sit on my back and fasten yourself on with your sash. Then we can fly away from the ugly mole and his gloomy rooms—far away over the mountains into warmer countries, where the sun shines more brightly than here;

At last, Thumbelina and the swallow came to a blue lake. By the side of it stood a palace.

where it is always summer and the flowers bloom in greater
beauty. Fly now with me, dear little Thumbelina. You saved
my life when I lay frozen in that dark dreary passage."

"Yes, I will go with you," said Thumbelina. And she seated
herself on the bird's back with her feet on his outstretched
wings, and tied her sash to one of his strongest feathers.

Then the swallow rose in the air and flew over forest and
over sea, high above the highest mountains, covered with
eternal snow. Thumbelina would have been frozen in the
cold air, but she crept under the bird's warm feathers,
keeping her little head uncovered so that she might admire
the beautiful lands over which they passed. At length they
reached the warm countries, where the sun shines brightly
and the sky seems much higher above the earth. Here on
the hedges and by the wayside grew purple, green, and
white grapes. Lemons and oranges hung from trees in the
woods, and the air was fragrant with myrtles and orange
blossoms. Beautiful children ran along the country lanes,
playing with large gay butterflies, and as the swallow flew
farther and farther, every place appeared still more lovely.

At last they came to a blue lake, and by the side of it,
shaded by trees of the deepest green, stood a palace of
dazzling white marble, built in the olden times. Vines clus-
tered round its lofty pillars and at the top were many
swallows' nests, and one of these was the home of the swallow
who carried Thumbelina.

"This is my house," said the swallow, "but it would not
do for you to live there. You would not be comfortable. You
must choose for yourself one of those lovely flowers, and
I will put you down upon it. And then you shall have
everything that you can wish to make you happy."

"That will be delightful," she said, and clapped her little
hands for joy.

A large marble pillar lay on the ground, which in falling
had been broken into three pieces. Between these pieces

grew the most beautiful large white flowers. So the swallow
flew down with Thumbelina and placed her on one of the
broad leaves. How surprised she was to see, in the middle
of the flower, a tiny little man, as white and transparent as
if he had been made of crystal! He had a gold crown on
his head, and delicate wings at his shoulders, and was not
much larger than Thumbelina herself. He was the angel of
the flower—for a tiny man or a tiny woman dwells in every
flower—and this was the king of them all.

"How beautiful he is!" whispered Thumbelina to the
swallow.

The little prince was at first quite frightened at the bird,
who was like a giant compared to such a delicate little
creature as himself. But when he saw Thumbelina, he was
delighted and thought her the prettiest little maiden he had
ever seen. He took the gold crown from his head, placed it
on hers, asked her name, and asked if she would be his wife
and the queen over all the flowers.

This certainly was a very different sort of husband from
the son of the toad, or the mole with his black velvet and
fur. So she said, "Yes," to the handsome prince. Then all
the flowers opened and out of each came a little lady or a
tiny lord, all so pretty it was quite a pleasure to look at them.
Each of them brought Thumbelina a present, but the best
gift was a pair of beautiful wings which had belonged to
a large white fly. And they fastened them to Thumbelina's
shoulders so that she might fly from flower to flower. Then
there was much rejoicing, and the little swallow, who sat
above them in his nest, was asked to sing a wedding song,
which he did as well as he could. But in his heart he felt
sad, for he was very fond of Thumbelina and would have
liked never to part from her again.

"You must not be called Thumbelina any more," said the
spirit of the flowers to her. "It is an ugly name and you
are so very pretty. We will call you Maia."

"Farewell, farewell," said the swallow, with a heavy heart, as he left the warm countries to fly back to Denmark. There he had a nest over the window of a house in which dwelt the writer of fairy tales. The swallow sang, "Tweet, tweet," and from his song came the whole story.

The Emperor's New Clothes

Many years ago there was an Emperor who was so excessively fond of new clothes that he spent all his money on them. He cared nothing about his soldiers, nor for the theatre, nor for driving in the woods except for the sake of showing off his new clothes. He had a costume for every hour in the day. Instead of saying as one does about any other king or emperor, "He is in his council chamber," the people here always said, "The Emperor is in his dressing room."

Life was very gay in the great town where he lived. Hosts of strangers came to visit it every day, and among them one day were two swindlers. They gave themselves out as weavers and said that they knew how to weave the most beautiful fabrics imaginable. Not only were the colors and patterns unusually fine, but the clothes that were made of this cloth had the peculiar quality of becoming invisible to every person who was not fit for the office he held, or who was impossibly dull.

"Those must be splendid clothes," thought the Emperor. "By wearing them I should be able to discover which men in my kingdom are unfitted for their posts. I shall distinguish the wise men from the fools. Yes, I certainly must order some of that stuff to be woven for me."

The Emperor paid the two swindlers a lot of money in advance, so that they might begin their work at once.

They did put up two looms and pretended to weave, but they had nothing whatever upon their shuttles. At the outset they asked for a quantity of the finest silk and the purest gold thread, all of which they put into their own bags while they worked away at the empty looms far into the night.

"I should like to know how those weavers are getting on with their cloth," thought the Emperor, but he felt a little queer when he reflected that anyone who was stupid or unfit for his post would not be able to see it. He certainly thought that he need have no fears for himself, but still he thought he would send somebody else first to see how it was getting on. Everybody in the town knew what wonderful power the stuff possessed, and everyone was anxious to see how stupid his neighbor was.

"I will send my faithful old minister to the weavers," thought the Emperor. "He will be best able to see how the stuff looks, for he is a clever man and no one fulfills his duties better than he does."

So the good old minister went into the room where the two swindlers sat working at the empty loom.

"Heaven help us," thought the old minister, opening his eyes very wide. "Why, I can't see a thing!" But he took care not to say so.

Both the swindlers begged him to be good enough to step a little nearer, and asked if he did not think it a good pattern and beautiful coloring. They pointed to the empty loom. The poor old minister stared as hard as he could, but he could not see anything, for of course there was nothing to see.

"Good heavens," thought he. "Is it possible that I am a fool? I have never thought so, and nobody must know it. Am I not fit for my post? It will never do to say that I cannot see the stuff."

"Well, sir, you don't say anything about the stuff," said the one who was pretending to weave.

"Oh, it is beautiful—quite charming," said the minister, looking through his spectacles. "Such a pattern and such colors! I will certainly tell the Emperor that the stuff pleases me very much."

"We are delighted to hear you say so," said the swindlers, and then they named all the colors and described the peculiar pattern. The old minister paid great attention to what they said, so as to be able to repeat it when he got home to the Emperor.

Then the swindlers went on to demand more money, more silk, and more gold, to be able to proceed with the weaving. But they put it all into their own pockets. Not a single strand was ever put into the loom, but they went on as before, weaving at the empty loom.

The Emperor soon sent another faithful official to see how the stuff was getting on and if it would soon be ready. The same thing happened to him as to the minister. He looked and looked, but as there was only the empty loom, he could see nothing at all.

"Is not this a beautiful piece of stuff?" said both the swindlers, showing and explaining the beautiful pattern and colors which were not there to be seen.

"I know I am no fool," thought the man, "so it must be that I am unfit for my good post. It is very strange, though. However, one must not let it appear." So he praised the stuff he did not see, and assured them of his delight in the beautiful colors and the originality of the design.

"It is absolutely charming," he said to the Emperor. Everybody in the town was talking about this splendid stuff.

Now the Emperor thought he would like to see it while it was still on the loom. So, accompanied by a number of selected courtiers, among whom were the two faithful officials who had already seen the imaginary stuff, he went to visit the crafty impostors, who were working away as hard as ever they could at the empty loom.

"It is magnificent," said both the honest officials. "Only see, Your Majesty, what a design! What colors!" And they pointed to the empty loom, for they each thought no doubt the others could see the stuff.

"What?" thought the Emperor. "I see nothing at all. This is terrible! Am I a fool? Am I not fit to be Emperor? Why, nothing worse could happen to me!"

"Oh, it is beautiful," said the Emperor. "It has my highest approval." And he nodded his satisfaction as he gazed at the empty loom. Nothing would induce him to say that he could not see anything.

The whole suite gazed and gazed, but saw nothing more than all the others. However, they all exclaimed with His Majesty, "It is very beautiful." And they advised him to wear a suit made of this wonderful cloth on the occasion of a great procession which was just about to take place. "Magnificent! Gorgeous! Excellent!" went from mouth to mouth. They were all equally delighted with it. The Emperor gave each of the rogues an order of knighthood to be worn in their buttonholes and the title of "Gentleman Weaver."

The swindlers sat up the whole night before the day on which the procession was to take place, burning sixteen candles, so that people might see how anxious they were to get the Emperor's new clothes ready. They pretended to take the stuff off the loom. They cut it out in the air with a huge pair of scissors, and they stitched away with needles without any thread in them.

At last they said, "Now the Emperor's new clothes are ready."

The Emperor with his grandest courtiers went to them himself, and both swindlers raised one arm in the air, as if they were holding something. They said, "See, these are the trousers. This is the coat. Here is the mantle," and so on.

"It is as light as a spider's web. One might think one had nothing on, but that is the very beauty of it."

"Yes," said all the courtiers, but they could not see anything, for there was nothing to see.

"Will Your Imperial Majesty be graciously pleased to take off your clothes?" said the impostors. "Then we may put on the new ones, along here before the great mirror."

The Emperor took off all his clothes, and the impostors pretended to give him one article of dress after the other of the new ones which they had pretended to make. They pretended to fasten something around his waist and to tie on something. This was the train, and the Emperor turned round and round in front of the mirror.

"How well His Majesty looks in the new clothes! How becoming they are!" cried all the people round. "What a design, and what colors! They are most gorgeous robes."

"The canopy is waiting outside which is to be carried over Your Majesty in the procession," said the master of the ceremonies.

"Well, I am quite ready," said the Emperor. "Don't the clothes fit well?" Then he turned round again in front of the mirror, so that he should seem to be looking at his grand things.

The chamberlains who were to carry the train stooped and pretended to lift it from the ground with both hands, and they walked along with their hands in the air. They dared not let it appear that they could not see anything.

Then the Emperor walked along in the procession under the gorgeous canopy, and everybody in the streets and at the windows exclaimed, "How beautiful the Emperor's new clothes are! What a splendid train! And they fit to perfection!" Nobody would let it appear that he could see nothing, for then he would not be fit for his post, or else he was a fool.

None of the Emperor's clothes had been so successful before.

" But he has got nothing on," said a little child.

" Oh, listen to the innocent," said its father. And one person whispered to the other what the child had said. "He has nothing on—a child says he has nothing on! "

" But he has nothing on! " at last cried all the people.

The Emperor writhed, for he knew it was true. But he thought, "The procession must go on now." So he held himself stiffer than ever, and the chamberlains held up the invisible train.

The Little Mermaid

Far out in the sea the water is as blue as the petals of the most beautiful cornflower, and as clear as the purest glass. But it is very deep, deeper than any cable will sound; many steeples must be placed one above the other to reach from the ground to the surface of the water. And down there live the sea people.

Now, you must not believe there is nothing down there but the naked sand; no—the strangest trees and plants grow there, so pliable in their stalks and leaves that at the least motion of the water they move just as if they had life. All fishes, great and small, glide among the twigs, just as here the birds do in the trees. In the deepest spot of all lies the sea king's castle: the walls are of coral, and the tall, Gothic windows of the clearest amber; shells form the roof, and they open and shut according as the water flows. It looks lovely, for in each shell lie gleaming pearls, a single one of which would have great value in a queen's diadem.

The sea king below there had been a widower for many years, while his old mother kept house for him. She was a clever woman, but proud of her rank, so she wore twelve oysters on her tail, while the other great people were only allowed to wear six. Beyond this she was deserving of great praise, especially because she was very fond of her grand-daughters, the little sea princesses. These were six pretty children; but the youngest was the most beautiful of all. Her skin was as clear and as fine as a rose leaf; her eyes were as blue as the deepest sea; but, like all the rest, she had no feet, for her body ended in a fishtail.

All day long they could play in the castle, down in the halls, where living flowers grew out of the walls. The great amber windows were opened, and then the fishes swam in to them, just as the swallows fly in to us when we open our windows; but the fishes swam straight up to the Princesses, ate out of their hands, and let themselves be stroked.

Outside the castle was a great garden with bright red and dark blue flowers; the fruit glowed like gold, and the flowers like flames of fire; and they continually kept moving their stalks and leaves. The earth itself was the finest sand, but blue as the flame of brimstone. A peculiar blue radiance lay upon everything down there: one would have thought oneself high in the air, with the canopy of heaven above and around, rather than at the bottom of the deep sea. During a calm the sun could be seen; it appeared like a purple flower, from which all light streamed out.

Each of the little Princesses had her own little place in the garden, where she might dig and plant at her good pleasure. One gave her flower bed the form of a whale; another thought it better to make hers like a little sea woman; but the youngest made hers quite round, like the sun, and had flowers which gleamed red as the sun itself. She was a strange child, quiet and thoughtful; and when the other sisters made a display of the beautiful things they had received out of wrecked ships, she would have nothing beyond the red flowers which resembled the sun, except a pretty marble statue. This was a figure of a charming boy, hewn out of white clear stone, which had sunk down to the bottom of the sea from a wreck. She planted a pink weeping willow beside this statue; the tree grew famously, and hung its fresh branches over the statue towards the blue sandy ground, where the shadow showed violet, and moved like the branches themselves; it seemed as if the ends of the branches and the roots were playing together and wished to kiss each other.

There was no greater pleasure for her than to hear of the world of men above them. The old grandmother had to tell all she knew of ships and towns, of men and animals. It seemed particularly beautiful to her that up on the earth the flowers shed fragrance, for they had none down at the bottom of the sea, and that the trees were green, and that the fishes which one saw there among the trees could sing so loud and clear that it was a pleasure to hear them. What the grandmother called fishes were the little birds; the Princess could not understand them in any other way, for she had never seen a bird.

" When you have reached your fifteenth year," said the grandmother, " you shall have leave to rise up out of the sea, to sit on the rocks in the moonlight, and to see the great ships as they sail by. Then you will see forests and towns! "

In the next year one of the sisters was fifteen years of age, but each of the others was one year younger than the next; so that the youngest had full five years to wait before she could come up from the bottom of the sea, and find how our world looked. But one promised to tell the others what she had seen and what she had thought the most beautiful on the first day of her visit; for their grandmother could not tell them enough—there was so much about which they wanted information.

No one was more anxious about these things than the youngest—just that one who had the longest time to wait, and who was always quiet and thoughtful. Many a night she stood by the open window, and looked up through the dark blue water at the fishes splashing with their fins and tails. Moon and stars she could see; they certainly shone quite faintly, but through the water they looked much larger than they appear in our eyes. When something like a black cloud passed among them, she knew that it was either a whale swimming over her head, or a ship with many people: they certainly did not think that a pretty little mermaid was standing down below stretching up her white hands toward the keel of their ship.

Now the eldest princess was fifteen years old, and might mount up to the surface of the sea.

When she came back, she had a hundred things to tell— but the finest thing, she said, was to lie in the moonshine on a sand bank in the quiet sea, and to look at the neighboring coast, with the large town, where the lights twinkled like a hundred stars, and to hear the music and the noise and clamor of carriages and men, to see the many church steeples, and to hear the sound of the bells. Just because she could not get up to these, she longed for them more than for anything.

O how the youngest sister listened! and afterwards when she stood at the open window and looked up through the dark-blue water, she thought of the great city with all its bustle and noise; and then she thought she could hear the church bells ringing, even down to the depth where she was.

In the following year, the second sister received permission to mount upward through the water and to swim whither she pleased. She rose up just as the sun was setting; and this spectacle, she said, was the most beautiful. The whole sky looked like gold, and as to the clouds, she could not properly describe their beauty. They sailed away over her head, purple and violet-colored, but far quicker than the clouds there flew a flight of wild swans, like a long white veil, over the water toward where the sun stood. She swam toward them; but the sun sank, and the roseate hue faded on the sea and in the clouds.

In the following year the next sister went up. She was the boldest of them all, and therefore she swam up a broad

stream that poured its waters into the sea. She saw glorious
green hills clothed with vines; palaces and castles shone
forth from amid splendid woods; she heard how all the birds
sang; and the sun shone so warm that she was often obliged
to dive under the water to cool her glowing face. In a little
bay she found a whole swarm of little mortals. They were
quite naked, and splashed about in the water: she wanted
to play with them, but they fled in affright, and a little black
animal came—it was a dog, but she had never seen a dog—
and it barked at her so terribly that she became frightened,
and tried to gain the open sea. But she could never forget
the glorious woods, the green hills, and the pretty children,
who could swim in the water, though they had not fishtails.

The fourth sister was not so bold: she remained out in the
midst of the wild sea, and declared that just there it was
most beautiful. One could see for many miles around, and
the sky above looked like a bell of glass. She had seen ships,
but only in the far distance—they looked like seagulls; and
the funny dolphins had thrown somersaults, and the great
whales spouted out water from their nostrils, so that it looked
like hundreds of fountains all around.

Now came the turn of the fifth sister. Her birthday came
in the winter, and so she saw what the others had not seen
the first time. The sea looked quite green, and great icebergs
were floating about; each one appeared like a pearl, she
said, and yet was much taller than the church steeples
built by men. They showed themselves in the strangest forms,
and shone like diamonds. She had seated herself upon one
of the greatest of all, and let the wind play with her long
hair; and all the sailing ships tacked about in a very rapid
way beyond where she sat: but toward evening the sky
became covered with clouds, it thundered and lightened, and
the black waves lifted the great ice blocks high up, and let
them glow in the red glare. On all the ships the sails were
reefed, and there was fear and anguish. But she sat quietly

upon her floating iceberg, and saw the forked blue flashes dart into the sea.

Each of the sisters, as she came up for the first time to the surface of the water, was delighted with the new and beautiful sights she saw; but as they now had permission, as grown-up girls, to go whenever they liked, it became indifferent to them. They wished themselves back again, and after a month had elapsed they said it was best of all down below, for there one felt so comfortably at home.

Many an evening hour the five sisters took one another by the arm and rose up in a row over the water. They had splendid voices, more charming than any mortal could have; and when a storm was approaching, so that they could apprehend that ships would go down, they swam on before the ships and sang lovely songs, which told how beautiful it was at the bottom of the sea, and exhorted the sailors not to be afraid to come down. But these could not understand the words, and thought it was the storm sighing; and they did not see the splendors below, for if the ships sank they were drowned, and came as corpses to the sea king's palace.

When the sisters thus rose up, arm in arm, in the evening time, through the water, the little sister stood all alone looking after them; and she felt as if she must weep; but the mermaid has no tears, and for this reason she suffers far more acutely.

"Of if I were only fifteen years old!" said she. "I know I shall love the world up there very much, and the people who live and dwell there."

At last she was really fifteen years old.

"Now, you see, you are grown up," said the grandmother, the old dowager. "Come, let me adorn you like your sisters."

And she put a wreath of white lilies in the little maid's hair, but each flower was half a pearl; and the old lady let eight great oysters attach themselves to the Princess' tail, in token of her high rank.

"But that hurts so!" said the little mermaid.

"Yes, pride must suffer pain," replied the old lady.

O how glad she would have been to shake off all the tokens of rank and lay aside the heavy wreath! Her red flowers in the garden suited her better; but she could not help it. "Farewell!" she said, and then she rose, light and clear as a water bubble, up through the sea.

The sun had just set when she lifted her head above the sea, but all the clouds still shone like roses and gold, and in the pale red sky the evening stars gleamed bright and beautiful. The air was mild and fresh, and the sea quite calm. There lay a great ship with three masts; one single sail only was set, for not a breeze stirred, and around in the shrouds and on the yards sat the sailors. There was music and singing, and as the evening closed in, hundreds of colored lanterns were lighted up, and looked as if the flags of every nation were waving in the air. The little mermaid swam straight to the cabin window, and each time the sea lifted her up, she could look through the panes, which were clear as crystal, and see many people standing within dressed in their best. But the handsomest of all was the young Prince with the great black eyes: he was certainly not much more than sixteen years old; it was his birthday, and that was the cause of all this feasting. The sailors were dancing upon deck, and when the young Prince came out, more than a hundred rockets rose into the air; they shone like day, so that the little mermaid was quite startled, and dived under the water; but soon she put out her head again, and then it seemed just as if all the stars of heaven were falling down upon her. She had never seen such fireworks. Great suns spurted fire all around, glorious fiery fishes flew up into the blue air, and everything was mirrored in the clear blue sea. The ship itself was so brightly lit up that every separate rope could be seen, and the people therefore appeared the more plainly. O how handsome the young Prince was! And he pressed the people's hands and smiled, while the music rang out in the glorious night.

It became late; but the little mermaid could not turn her eyes from the ship and from the beautiful Prince. The colored lanterns were extinguished, rockets ceased to fly into the air, and no more cannons were fired; but there was a murmuring and a buzzing deep down in the sea; and she sat on the water, swaying up and down, so that she could look into the cabin. But as the ship got more way, one sail after another was spread. And now the waves rose higher, great clouds came up, and in the distance there was lightning. O! it was going to be fearful weather, therefore the sailors furled the sails. The great ship flew in swift career over the wild sea: the waters rose up like great black mountains, which wanted to roll over the masts; but like a swan the ship dived into the valleys between these high waves, and then let itself be lifted on high again. To the little mermaid this seemed merry sport, but to the sailors it appeared very differently. The ship groaned and creaked; the thick planks were bent by the heavy blows; the sea broke into the ship; the mainmast snapped in two like a thin reed; and the ship lay over on her side, while the water rushed into the hold. Now the little mermaid saw that the people were in peril; she herself was obliged to take care to avoid the beams and fragments of the ship which were floating about on the waters. One moment it was so pitch dark that not a single object could be described, but when it lightened it became so bright that she could distinguish every one on board. She looked particularly for the young Prince, and when the ship parted she saw him sink into the sea. Then she was very glad, for now he would come down to her. But then she remembered that people could not live in the water, and that when he got down to her father's palace he would certainly be dead. No, he must not die: so she swam about among the beams and planks that strewed the surface, quite forgetting that one of them might have crushed her. Diving down deep under the water, she again rose high up among the waves, and in this way she at last came to the Prince, who could scarcely swim longer in that stormy sea. His arms and legs began to fail him, his beautiful eyes closed, and he would have died had the little mermaid not come. She held his head up over the water, and then allowed the waves to carry her and him whither they listed.

When the morning came the storm had passed by. Of the ship not a fragment was to be seen. The sun came up red and shining out of the water; it was as if its beams brought back the hue of life to the cheeks of the Prince, but his eyes remained closed. The mermaid kissed his high, fair forehead and put back his wet hair, and he seemed to her to be like the marble statue in her little garden: she kissed him again and hoped that he might live.

Now she saw in front of her the dry land—high blue mountains, on whose summits the white snow gleamed as if swans were lying there. Down on the coast were glorious green forests, and a building—she could not tell whether it was a church or a convent—stood there. In its garden grew orange and citron trees, and high palms waved in front of the gate. The sea formed a little bay there; it was quite calm, but very deep. Straight toward the rock where the fine white sand had been cast up, she swam with the handsome Prince, and laid him upon the sand, taking especial care that his head was raised in the warm sunshine.

Now all the bells rang in the great white building, and many young girls came walking through the garden. Then the little mermaid swam farther out between some high stones that stood up out of the water, laid some sea foam upon her hair and neck, so that no one could see her little countenance, and then she watched to see who would come to the poor Prince.

In a short time a young girl went that way. She seemed

to be much startled, but only for a moment; then she brought more people, and the mermaid perceived that the Prince came back to life, and that he smiled at all around him. But he did not cast a smile at her: he did not know that she had saved him. And she felt very sorrowful; and when he was led away into the great building, she dived mournfully under the water and returned to her father's palace.

She had always been gentle and melancholy, but now she became much more so. Her sisters asked her what she had seen the first time she rose up to the surface, but she would tell them nothing.

Many an evening and many a morning she went up to the place where she had left the Prince. She saw how the fruits of the garden grew ripe and were gathered; she saw how the snow melted on the high mountain; but she did not see the Prince, and so she always returned home more sorrowful still. Then her only comfort was to sit in her little garden, and to wind her arm round the beautiful marble statue that resembled the Prince; but she did not tend her flowers; they grew as if in a wilderness over the paths, and trailed their long leaves and stalks up into the branches of trees, so that it became quite dark there.

At last she could endure it no longer, and told all to one of her sisters, and then the others heard of it too; but nobody knew of it beyond these and a few other mermaids, who told the secret to their intimate friends. One of these knew who the Prince was; she too had seen the festival on board the ship; and she announced whence he came and where his kingdom lay.

" Come, little sister! " said the other Princesses; and, linking their arms together, they rose up in a long row out of the sea, at the place where they knew the Prince's palace lay.

This palace was built of a kind of bright yellow stone, with great marble staircases, one of which led directly down into the sea. Over the roof rose splendid gilt cupolas, and between the pillars which surrounded the whole dwelling, stood marble statues which looked as if they were alive. Through the clear glass in the high windows one looked into the glorious halls, where costly silk hangings and tapestries were hung up, and all the walls were decked with splendid pictures, so that it was a perfect delight to see them. In the midst of the greatest of these halls a great fountain plashed; its jets shot high up toward the glass dome in the ceiling, through which the sun shone down upon the water and upon the lovely plants growing in the great basin.

Now she knew where he lived, and many an evening and many a night she spent there on the water. She swam far closer to the land than any of the others would have dared to venture; indeed, she went quite up the narrow channel under the splendid marble balcony, which threw a broad shadow upon the water. Here she sat and watched the young Prince, who thought himself quite alone in the bright moonlight.

Many an evening she saw him sailing, amid the sounds of music, in his costly boat with the waving flags; she peeped up through the green reeds, and when the wind caught her silver-white veil, and any one saw it, he thought it was a white swan spreading out its wings.

Many a night when the fishermen were on the sea with their torches, she heard much good told of the young Prince; and she rejoiced that she had saved his life when he was driven about, half dead, on the wild billows: she thought how quietly his head had reclined on her bosom, and how heartily she had kissed him; but he knew nothing of it, and could not even dream of her.

More and more she began to love mankind, and more and more she wished to be able to wander about among those whose world seemed far larger than her own. For they could fly over the sea in ships, and mount up the high hills far above the clouds, and the lands they possessed stretched out in woods and fields farther than her eyes could reach. There was much she wished to know, but her sisters could not answer all her questions; therefore she applied to the old grandmother; and the old lady knew the upper world, which she rightly called "the countries above the sea," very well.

"If people are not drowned," asked the little mermaid, "can they live forever? Do they not die as we die down here in the sea?"

"Yes," replied the old lady. "They too must die, and their life is even shorter than ours. We can live to be three hundred years old, but when we cease to exist here, we are turned into foam on the surface of the water, and have not even a grave down here among those we love. We have not an immortal soul; we never receive another life; we are like the green seaweed, which, when once cut through, can never bloom again. Men, on the contrary, have a soul which lives forever, which lives on after the body has become dust; it mounts up through the clear air, up to all the shining stars! As we rise up out of the waters and behold all the lands of the earth, so they rise up to unknown glorious places which we can never see."

"Why did we not receive an immortal soul?" asked the little mermaid, sorrowfully. "I would gladly give all the hundreds of years I have to live to be a human being only for one day, and to have a hope of partaking the heavenly kingdom."

"You must not think of that," replied the old lady. "We feel ourselves far more happy and far better than mankind yonder."

"Then I am to die and be cast as foam upon the sea, not hearing the music of the waves, nor seeing the pretty flowers and the red sun? Can I not do anything to win an immortal soul?"

"No!" answered the grandmother. "Only if a man were to love you so that you should be more to him than father

or mother; if he should cling to you with his every thought
and with all his love, and let the priest lay his right hand
in yours with a promise of faithfulness here and in all
eternity, then his soul would be imparted to your body, and
you would receive a share of the happiness of mankind. He
would give a soul to you and yet retain his own. But that
can never come to pass. What is considered beautiful here
in the sea—the fishtail—they would consider ugly on the
earth: they don't understand it; there one must have two
clumsy supports which they call legs, to be called beautiful."

Then the little mermaid sighed and looked mournfully
upon her fishtail.

"Let us be glad!" said the old lady. "Let us dance and
leap in the three hundred years we have to live. That is
certainly long enough; after that we can rest ourselves all
the better. This evening we shall have a court ball."

It was a splendid sight, such as is never seen on earth.
The walls and the ceiling of the great dancing-saloon were
of thick but transparent glass. Several hundreds of huge
shells, pink and grass-green, stood on each side in rows,
filled with a blue fire which lit up the whole hall and shone
through the walls, so that the sea without was quite lit up;
one could see all the innumerable fishes, great and small,
swimming toward the glass walls; of some the scales gleamed
with purple, while in others they shone like silver and gold.
Through the midst of the hall flowed a broad stream, and
on this the sea men and sea women danced to their own
charming songs. Such beautiful voices the people of the
earth have not. The little mermaid sang the most sweetly
of all, and the whole court applauded with hands and tails,
and for a moment she felt gay in her heart, for she
knew she had the loveliest voice of all in the sea or on the
earth. But soon she thought again of the world above her;
she could not forget the charming Prince, or her sorrow at
not having an immortal soul like his. Therefore she crept

out of her father's palace, and while everything within was joy and gladness, she sat melancholy in her little garden. Then she heard the bugle horn sounding through the waters, and thought, "Now he is certainly sailing above, he on whom my wishes hang, and in whose hand I should like to lay my life's happiness. I will dare everything to win him and an immortal soul. While my sisters dance yonder in my father's palace, I will go to the sea witch of whom I have always been so much afraid: perhaps she can counsel and help me."

Now the little mermaid went out of her garden to the foaming whirlpools behind which the sorceress dwelt. She had never traveled that way before. No flowers grew there, no sea grass; only the naked gray sand stretched out toward the whirlpools, where the water rushed round like roaring millwheels and tore down everything it seized into the deep. Through the midst of these rushing whirlpools she was obliged to pass to get into the domain of the witch; and for a long way there was no other road except one which led over warm gushing mud: this the witch called her turf moor. Behind it lay her house in the midst of a singular forest, in which all the trees and bushes were polyps—half-animals, half-plants. They looked like hundred-headed snakes growing up out of the earth. All the branches were long, slimy arms, with fingers like supple worms, and they moved limb by limb from the root to the farthest point; all that they could seize on in the water they held fast and did not let it go. The little mermaid stopped in front of them quite frightened; her heart beat with fear, and she was near turning back; but then she thought of the Prince and the human soul, and her courage came back again. She bound her long, flying hair closely around her head, so that the polyps might not seize it. She put her hands together on her breast, and then shot forward, as a fish shoots through the water, among the ugly polyps, which stretched out their supple arms and fingers

after her. She saw that each of them held something it had
seized with hundreds of little arms, like strong iron bands.
People who had perished at sea, and had sunk deep down,
looked forth as white skeletons from among the polyps' arms;
ships' oars and chests they also held fast, and skeletons of
land animals, and a little sea woman whom they had caught
and strangled; and this seemed the most terrible of all to our
little Princess.

Now she came to a great marshy place in the wood, where
fat water snakes rolled about, showing their ugly cream-
colored bodies. In the midst of this marsh was a house built
of white bones of shipwrecked men; there sat the sea witch,
feeding a toad out of her mouth, just as a person might feed
a little canary with sugar. She called the ugly fat water
snakes her little chickens, and allowed them to crawl upward
and all about her.

"I know what you want," said the sea witch. "It is stupid
of you, but you shall have your way, for it will bring you
to grief, my pretty Princess. You want to get rid of your
fishtail, and to have two supports instead of it, like those the
people of the earth walk with, so that the young Prince may
fall in love with you, and you may get an immortal soul."
And with this the Witch laughed loudly and disagreeably, so
that the toad and the water snakes tumbled down to the
ground, where they crawled about. "You come just in time,"
said the Witch: "after tomorrow at sunrise I could not help
you until another year had gone by. I will prepare a draught
for you, with which you must swim to land tomorrow before
the sun rises, and seat yourself there and drink it; then your
tail will shrivel up and become what the people of the earth
call legs; but it will hurt you—it will seem as if you were
cut with a sharp sword. All who see you will declare you
to be the prettiest human being they ever beheld. You will
keep your graceful walk; no dancer will be able to move so
lightly as you; but every step you take will be as if you trod

upon sharp knives, and as if your blood must flow. If you will bear all this, I can help you."

"Yes!" said the little mermaid, with a trembling voice; and she thought of the Prince and the immortal soul.

"But remember," said the Witch, "when you have once received a human form, you can never be a mermaid again; you can never return through the water to your sisters, or to your father's palace; and if you do not win the Prince's love, so that he forgets father and mother for your sake, is attached to you heart and soul, and tells the priest to join your hands, you will not receive an immortal soul. On the first morning after he has married another, your heart will break, and you will become foam on the water."

"I will do it," said the little mermaid; but she became as pale as death.

"But you must pay me, too," said the Witch; "and it is not a trifle that I ask. You have the finest voice of all here at the bottom of the water; with that you think to enchant him; but this voice you must give to me. The best thing you possess I will have for my costly draught! I must give you my own blood in it, so that the draught may be sharp as a two-edged sword."

"But if you take away my voice," said the little mermaid, "what will remain to me?"

"Your beautiful form," replied the Witch, "your graceful walk, and your speaking eyes: with those you can take captive a human heart. Well, have you lost your courage? Put out your little tongue, and then I will cut it off for my payment, and then you shall have the strong draught."

"It shall be so," said the little mermaid.

And the Witch put on her pot to brew the draught.

"Cleanliness is a good thing," said she; and she cleaned out the pot with the snakes, which she tied up in a big knot; then she scratched herself, and let her black blood drop into it. The stream rose up in the strangest forms, enough to frighten the beholder. Every moment the Witch threw something else into the pot; and when it boiled thoroughly, there was a sound like the weeping of a crocodile. At last the draught was ready. It looked like the purest water.

"There you have it," said the Witch.

And she cut off the little mermaid's tongue, so that now the Princess was dumb, and could neither sing nor speak.

She could see her father's palace. The torches were extinguished in the great hall, and they were certainly sleeping within, but she did not dare to go to them, now that she was dumb and was about to quit them forever. She felt as if her heart would burst with sorrow. She crept into the garden, took a flower from each bed of her sisters, blew a thousand kisses toward the palace, and rose up through the dark blue sea.

The sun had not yet risen when she beheld the Prince's castle, and mounted the splendid marble staircase. The moon shone beautifully clear. The little mermaid drank the burning sharp draught, and it seemed as if a two-edged sword went through her delicate body. She fell down in a swoon, and lay as if she were dead. When the sun shone out over the sea she awoke, and felt a sharp pain; but just before her stood the handsome young Prince. He fixed his coal-black eyes upon her, so that she cast down her own, and then she perceived that her fishtail was gone, and that she had the prettiest pair of white feet a little girl could have. But she had no clothes, so she shrouded herself in her long hair. The Prince asked how she came there; and she looked at him mildly, but very mournfully, with her dark-blue eyes, for she could not speak. Then he took her by the hand, and led her into the castle. Each step she took was, as the Witch had told her, as if she had been treading on pointed needles and knives, but she bore it gladly. At the Prince's right hand she moved on, light as a soap bubble, and he, like all the rest, was astonished at her graceful, swaying movements.

She now received splendid clothes of silk and muslin. In the castle she was the most beautiful creature to be seen; but she was dumb, and could neither sing nor speak. Lovely slaves, dressed in silk and gold, stepped forward, and sang before the Prince and his royal parents; one sang more charmingly than all the rest, and the Prince smiled at her and clapped his hands. Then the little mermaid became sad; she knew that she herself had sung far more sweetly, and thought—

" O! that he only knew I had given away my voice forever to be with him! "

Now the slaves danced pretty waving dances to the loveliest music; then the little mermaid lifted her beautiful white arms, stood on the tips of her toes, and glided dancing over the floor as no one had yet danced. At each movement her beauty became more apparent, and her eyes spoke more directly to the heart than the songs of the slaves.

All were delighted, and especially the Prince, who called her his little foundling; and she danced again and again, although every time she touched the earth it seemed as if she were treading upon sharp knives. The Prince said that she should always remain with him, and she received permission to sleep on a velvet cushion before his door.

He had a page's dress made for her, that she might accompany him on horseback. They rode through the blooming woods, where the green boughs swept their shoulders, and the little birds sang in the fresh leaves. She climbed with the Prince up the high mountains, and although her delicate feet bled so that even the others could see it, she laughed at it herself, and followed him until they saw the clouds sailing beneath them, like a flock of birds traveling to distant lands.

At home in the Prince's castle, when the others slept at night, she went out on to the broad marble steps. It cooled

her burning feet to stand in the cold sea water, and then
she thought of the dear ones in the deep.

Once, in the nighttime, her sisters came, arm in arm. Sadly
they sang as they floated above the water; and she beckoned
to them, and they recognized her, and told her how she had
grieved them all. Then she visited them every night; and
once she saw in the distance her old grandmother, who had
not been above the surface for many years, and the sea king
with his crown upon his head. They stretched out their hands
toward her, but did not venture so near the land as her
sisters.

Day by day the Prince grew more fond of her. He loved
her as one loves a dear, good child, but it never came into
his head to make her his wife; and yet she must become
his wife, or she would not receive an immortal soul, and
would have to become foam on the sea on his marriage
morning.

"Do you not love me best of them all?" the eyes of the
little mermaid seemed to say, when he took her in his arms
and kissed her fair forehead.

"Yes, you are the dearest to me!" said the Prince, "for
you have the best heart of them all. You are the most devoted
to me, and are like a young girl whom I once saw, but whom
I certainly shall not find again. I was on board a ship which
was wrecked. The waves threw me ashore near a holy temple,
where several young girls performed the service. The
youngest of them found me by the shore and saved my life.
I only saw her twice: she was the only one in the world I
could love; but you chase her picture out of my mind, you
are so like her. She belongs to the holy temple, and therefore
my good fortune has sent you to me. We will never part!"

"Ah! he does not know that I saved his life," thought the
little mermaid. "I carried him over the sea to the wood
where the temple stands. I sat there under the foam and
looked to see if any one would come. I saw the beautiful

girl whom he loves better than me." And the mermaid sighed deeply—she could not weep. "The maiden belongs to the holy temple," she said, "and will never come out into the world—they will meet no more. I am with him and see him every day; I will cherish him, love him, give up my life for him."

But now they said that the Prince was to marry, and that the beautiful daughter of a neighboring King was to be his wife, and that was why such a beautiful ship was being prepared. The story was, that the Prince traveled to visit the land of the neighboring King, but it was done that he might see the King's daughter. A great company was to go with him. The little mermaid shook her head and smiled; she knew the Prince's thoughts far better than any of the others.

"I must travel," he had said to her; "I must see the beautiful Princess: my parents desire it, but they do not wish to compel me to bring her home as my bride. I cannot love her. She is not like the beautiful maiden in the temple whom you resemble. If I were to choose a bride, I would rather choose you, my dear dumb foundling with the speaking eyes."

And he kissed her red lips and played with her long hair, so that she dreamed of happiness and of an immortal soul.

"You are not afraid of the sea, my dumb child?" said he, when they stood on the superb ship which was to carry him to the country of the neighboring King; and he told her of storm and calm, of strange fishes in the deep, and of what the divers had seen there. And she smiled at his tales, for she knew better than any one what happened at the bottom of the sea.

In the moonlight night, when all were asleep, except the steersman who stood by the helm, she sat on the side of the ship gazing down through the clear water. She fancied she saw her father's palace. High on the battlements stood her old grandmother, with the silver crown on her head, and looking

through the rushing tide up to the vessel's keel. Then her
sisters came forth over the water, and looked mournfully at
her and wrung their white hands. She beckoned to them,
smiled, and wished to tell them that she was well and happy;
but the cabin boy approached her and her sisters dived down,
so that he thought the white objects he had seen were foam
on the surface of the water.

The next morning the ship sailed into the harbor of the
neighboring King's splendid city. All the church bells
sounded, and from the high towers the trumpets were blown,
while the soldiers stood there with flying colors and flashing
bayonets. Each day brought some festivity with it; balls and
entertainments followed one another; but the Princess was
not yet there. People said she was being educated in a holy
temple far away, where she was learning every royal virtue.
At last she arrived.

The little mermaid was anxious to see the beauty of the
Princess, and was obliged to acknowledge it. A more lovely
apparition she had never beheld. The Princess' skin was pure
and clear, and behind the long dark eyelashes there smiled a
pair of faithful, dark-blue eyes.

" You are the lady who saved me when I lay like a corpse
upon the shore! " said the Prince; and he folded his blushing
bride to his heart. " O, I am too, too happy! " he cried to the
little mermaid. " The best hope I could have is fulfilled. You
will rejoice at my happiness, for you are the most devoted
to me of them all! "

And the little mermaid kissed his hand; and it seemed
already to her as if her heart was broken, for his wedding
morning was to bring death to her, and change her into foam
on the sea.

All the church bells were ringing, and heralds rode about
the streets announcing the betrothal. On every altar fragrant
oil was burning in gorgeous lamps of silver. The priests swung
their censers, and bride and bridegroom laid hand in hand,

and received the bishop's blessing. The little mermaid was dressed in cloth of gold, and held up the bride's train; but her ears heard nothing of the festive music, her eye marked not the holy ceremony; she thought of the night of her death, and of all that she had lost in this world.

On the same evening the bride and bridegroom went on board the ship. The cannon roared, all the flags waved; in the midst of the ship a costly tent of gold and purple, with the most beautiful cushions, had been set up, and there the married pair were to sleep in the cool, still night.

The sails swelled in the wind, and the ship glided smoothly and lightly over the clear sea. When it grew dark, colored lamps were lighted and the sailors danced merry dances on deck. The little mermaid thought of the first time when she had risen up out of the sea, and beheld a similar scene of splendor and joy; and she joined in the whirling dance, and flitted on as the swallow flits away when he is pursued; and all shouted and admired her, for she had danced so prettily. Her delicate feet were cut as if with knives, but she did not feel it, for her heart was wounded far more painfully. She knew this was the last evening on which she should see him for whom she had left her friends and her home, and had given up her beautiful voice, and had suffered unheard-of pains every day, while he was utterly unconscious of all. It was the last evening she should breathe the same air with him, and behold the starry sky and the deep sea; and everlasting night without thought or dream awaited her, for she had no soul, and could win none. And everything was merriment and gladness on the ship till past midnight, and she laughed and danced with thoughts of death in her heart. The Prince kissed his beautiful bride, and she played with his raven hair, and hand in hand they went to rest in the splendid tent. It became quiet on the ship; only the helmsman stood by the helm, and the little mermaid leaned her white arms upon the bulwark and gazed out toward the east for

the morning dawn—the first ray, she knew, would kill her.
Then she saw her sisters rising out of the flood; they were
pale, like herself; their long, beautiful hair no longer waved
in the wind; it had been cut off.

"We have given it to the Witch, that we might bring you
help, so that you may not die tonight. She has given us a
knife; here it is—look! how sharp! Before the sun rises you
must thrust it into the heart of the Prince, and when the
warm blood falls upon your feet they will grow together
again into a fishtail, and you will become a mermaid again,
and come back to us, and live your three hundred years
before you become dead salt sea foam. Make haste! He or
you must die before the sun rises! Our old grandmother
mourns so that her white hair has fallen off, as ours did
under the Witch's scissors. Kill the Prince and come back!
Make haste! Do you see that red streak in the sky? In a few
minutes the sun will rise, and you must die! "

And they gave a very mournful sigh, and vanished beneath
the waves. The little mermaid drew back the curtain from
the tent, and saw the beautiful bride lying with her head
on the Prince's breast; and she bent down and kissed his
brow, and gazed up to the sky where the morning red was
gleaming brighter and brighter; then she looked at the sharp
knife, and again fixed her eyes upon the Prince, who in his
sleep murmured his bride's name. She only was in his
thoughts, and the knife trembled in the mermaid's hand. But
then she flung it far away into the waves—they gleamed red
where it fell, and it seemed as if drops of blood spurted
up out of the water. Once more she looked with half-
extinguished eyes upon the Prince; then she threw herself
from the ship into the sea, and felt her frame dissolving into
foam.

Now the sun rose up out of the sea. The rays fell mild and
warm upon the cold sea foam, and the little mermaid felt
nothing of death. She saw the bright sun, and over her head

sailed hundreds of glorious ethereal beings—she could see them through the white sails of the ship and the red clouds of the sky; their speech was melody, but of such a spiritual kind that no human ear could hear it, just as no human eye could see them; without wings they floated through the air. The little mermaid found that she had a frame like these, and was rising more and more out of the foam.

"Whither am I going?" she asked; and her voice sounded like that of the other beings, so spiritual, that no earthly music could be compared to it.

"To the daughters of the air!" replied the others. "A mermaid has no immortal soul, and can never gain one, except she win the love of a mortal. Her eternal existence depends upon the power of another. The daughters of the air have likewise no immortal soul, but they can make themselves one through good deeds. We fly to the hot countries, where the close, pestilent air kills men, and there we bring coolness. We disperse the fragrance of the flowers through the air, and spread refreshment and health. After we have striven for three hundred years to accomplish all the good we can bring about, we receive an immortal soul, and take part in the eternal happiness of men. You, poor little mermaid, have striven with your whole heart after the goal we pursue; you have suffered and endured; you have by good works raised yourself to the world of spirits, and can gain an immortal soul after three hundred years."

And the little mermaid lifted her glorified eyes toward God's sun, and for the first time she felt them fill with tears. On the ship there was again life and noise. She saw the Prince and his bride searching for her; then they looked mournfully at the pearly foam, as if they knew that she had thrown herself into the waves. Invisible, she kissed the forehead of the bride, fanned the Prince, and mounted with the other children of the air on the rosy cloud which floated through the ether. After three hundred years we shall thus float into Paradise!

" And we may even get there sooner," whispered a daughter of the air. "Invisibly we float into the houses of men where children are, and for every day on which we find a good child that brings joy to its parents and deserves their love, our time of probation is shortened. The child does not know when we fly through the room; and when we smile with joy at the child's conduct, a year is counted off from the three hundred; but when we see a naughty or a wicked child, we shed tears of grief, and for every tear a day is added to our time of trial."

The Wild Swans

Far away, where the swallows take refuge in winter, lived a King who had eleven sons and one daughter, Elise. The eleven brothers—they were all princes—used to go to school with stars on their breasts and swords at their sides. They wrote upon golden slates with diamond pencils, and could read just as well without a book as with one, so there was no mistake about their being real princes. Their sister Elise sat upon a little footstool of looking glass, and she had a picture book which had cost the half of a kingdom. Oh, these children were very happy, but it was not to last thus forever.

Their father, who was King over all the land, married a wicked Queen who was not at all kind to the poor children. They found that out on the first day. All was festive at the castle, but when the children wanted to play at having company, instead of letting them have all the cakes and baked apples they wanted, she would only let them have some sand in a teacup, and said they must make-believe.

In the following week she sent little Elise into the country to board with some peasants, and it did not take her long to make the King believe so many bad things about the boys that he cared no more about them.

"Fly out into the world and look after yourselves," said the wicked Queen. "You shall fly about like birds without voices."

But she could not make things as bad for them as she would have liked: they turned into eleven beautiful wild swans. They flew out of the palace window with a weird scream, right across the park and the woods.

It was very early in the morning when they came to the place where their sister Elise was sleeping in the peasant's house. They hovered over the roof of the house, turning and twisting their long necks and flapping their wings, but no one either heard or saw them. They had to fly away again, and they soared up towards the clouds, far out into the wide world, and they settled in a big dark wood which stretched down to the shore.

Poor little Elise stood in the peasant's room playing with a green leaf, for she had no other toys. She made a little hole in it which she looked through at the sun, and it seemed to her as if she saw her brothers' bright eyes. Every time the warm sunbeams shone upon her cheek it reminded her of their kisses.

One day passed just like another. When the wind whistled through the rose hedges outside the house, it whispered to the roses, "Who can be prettier than you are?" But the roses shook their heads and answered, "Elise." And when the old woman sat in the doorway reading her psalms, the wind turned over the leaves and said to the book, "Who can be more pious than you?" "Elise," answered the book. Both the roses and the book of psalms spoke only the truth.

She was to go home when she was fifteen, but when the Queen saw how pretty she was, she got very angry and her heart was filled with hatred. She would willingly have turned her into a wild swan like her brothers, but she did not dare to do it at once, because the King wanted to see his daughter.

The Queen always went to the bath in the early morning. It was built of marble and adorned with soft cushions and beautiful carpets.

She took three toads, kissed them, and said to the first,

"Sit upon Elise's head when she comes to the bath, so that she may become sluggish like yourself. Sit upon her forehead," she said to the second, "that she many become ugly like you, and then her father won't know her. Rest upon her heart," she whispered to the third. "Let an evil spirit come over her which may be a burden to her."

Then she put the toads into the clean water and a green tinge immediately came over it. She called Elise, undressed her, and made her go into the bath. When she ducked under the water, one of the toads got among her hair, the other got onto her forehead, and the third onto her bosom. But when she stood up, three scarlet poppies floated on the water! Had the creatures not been poisonous, and been kissed by the sorceress, they would have been changed into crimson roses. Yet they became flowers from merely having rested a moment on her head and her heart. She was far too good and innocent for the sorcery to have any power over her.

When the wicked Queen saw this, she rubbed her over with walnut juice and smeared her face with some evil-smelling salve. She also matted up her beautiful hair. It would have been impossible to recognize pretty Elise. When her father saw her, he was quite horrified and said that she could not be his daughter. Nobody would have anything to say to her, except the yard dog and the swallows, but they were poor dumb animals whose opinion went for nothing.

Poor Elise wept and thought of her eleven brothers who were all lost. She crept sadly out of the palace and wandered about all day, over meadows and marshes and into a big forest. She did not know in the least where she wanted to go, but she felt very sad and longed for her brothers, who, no doubt, like herself had been driven out of the palace.

She made up her mind to go and look for them, but she had only been in the wood for a short time when night fell. She had quite lost her way, so she lay down upon the soft moss, said her evening prayer, and rested her head on a little hillock. It was very still and the air was mild. Hundreds of glowworms shone around her on the grass and in the marsh like green fire. When she gently moved one of the branches over her head, the little shining insects fell over her like a shower of stars.

She dreamt about her brothers all night long. Again they were children playing together. They wrote upon the golden slates with their diamond pencils, and she looked at the picture book which had cost half a kingdom. But they no longer wrote strokes and noughts upon their slates as they used to do. No, they wrote down all their boldest exploits and everything that they had seen and experienced. Everything in the picture book was alive. The birds sang, and the people walked out of the book and spoke to Elise and her brothers. When she turned over a page they skipped back into their places again, so that there should be no confusion among the pictures.

When she woke the sun was already high. It is true she could not see it very well through the thick branches of the lofty forest trees, but the sunbeams cast a golden shimmer around beyond the forest. There was a fresh delicious scent of grass and herbs in the air, and the birds were almost ready to perch upon her shoulders. She could hear the splashing of water, for there were many springs around, which all flowed into a pond with a lovely sandy bottom. It was surrounded with thick bushes but there was one place which the stags had trampled down, and Elise passed through the opening to the waterside. It was so transparent that, had not the branches been moved by the breeze, she must have thought that they were painted on the bottom—so plainly was every leaf reflected, both those on which the sun played and those which were in shade.

When she saw her own face, she was quite frightened to see it so brown and ugly. But when she wet her little hand and rubbed her eyes and forehead, her white skin shone through again. Then she took off all her clothes and went into the fresh water. A more beautiful royal child than she could not be found in all the world.

When she had put on her clothes again and plaited her long hair, she went to a sparkling spring and drank some of the water out of the hollow of her hand. Then she wandered further into the wood, though she had not the least idea where she was going. She thought of her brothers, and she thought of a merciful God who would not forsake her. He lets the wild crab apples grow to feed the hungry, and He showed her a tree the branches of which were bending beneath their weight of fruit. Here she made her midday meal. Then, having put props under the branches, she walked on into the thickest part of the forest. It was so quiet that she heard her own footsteps. She heard every little withered leaf which bent under her feet. Not a bird was to be seen. Not a ray of sunlight pierced the leafy branches, and the tall trunks were so close together that when she looked before her it seemed as if a thick fence of heavy beams hemmed her in on every side. The solitude was such as she had never known before.

It was a very dark night. Not a single glowworm sparkled in the marsh. Sadly she lay down to sleep, and it seemed to her as if the branches above her parted asunder, and that the Saviour looked down upon her with His loving eyes and that little angels' heads peeped out above His head and under His arms.

When she woke in the morning, she was not sure if she had dreamt this or whether it was really true.

She walked a little further when she met an old woman with a basket full of berries, of which she gave her some. Elise asked if she had seen eleven princes ride through the wood.

"No," said the old woman. "But yesterday I saw eleven

swans with golden crowns upon their heads, swimming in the stream close by there."

She led Elise a little further to a slope, at the foot of which the stream meandered. The trees on either bank stretched out their rich leafy branches towards each other. And where their natural growth did not let them reach each other, they had torn their roots out of the ground and leaned over the water in order to interlace their branches.

Elise said good-bye to the old woman and walked along by the river till it flowed out into the great open sea.

The beautiful open sea lay before the maiden, but not a sail was to be seen on it, nor a single boat. How was she ever to get any further? She looked at the numberless little pebbles on the beach. They were all worn quite round by the water. Glass, iron, stone—whatever was washed up—had taken their shapes from the water, which yet was much softer than her little hand.

"With all its rolling, it is untiring, and everything hard is smoothed down," she said. "I will be just as untiring. Thank you for your lesson, you clear rolling waves! Sometime, so my heart tells me, you will bear me to my beloved brothers."

Eleven white swans' feathers were lying on the seaweed. She picked them up and made a bunch of them. There were still drops of water on them, but whether these were dew or tears no one could tell. It was very lonely there by the shore, but she did not feel it, for the sea was everchanging. There were more changes on it in the course of a few hours than could be seen on an inland fresh-water lake in a year. If a big black cloud arose, it was just as if the sea wanted to say, "I can look black too." And then the wind blew up and the waves showed their white crests. But if the clouds were red and the wind dropped, the sea looked like a rose leaf, now white, now green. But however still it was, there was always a little gentle motion just by the shore. The water rose and fell softly like the bosom of a sleeping child.

When the sun was about to go down, Elise saw eleven wild swans with golden crowns upon their heads flying towards the shore. They flew in a swaying line one behind the other, like a white ribbon streamer. Elise climbed up onto the bank and hid behind a bush. The swans settled close by her and flapped their great white wings.

As soon as the sun had sunk beneath the water the swans shed their feathers and became eleven handsome princes. They were Elise's brothers. Although they had altered a good deal, she knew them at once. She felt that they must be her brothers and she sprang into their arms, calling them by name. They were delighted when they recognized their little sister who had grown so big and beautiful. They laughed and cried and told each other how wickedly their stepmother had treated them all.

"We brothers," said the eldest, "have to fly about in the guise of swans as long as the sun is above the horizon. When it goes down we regain our human shapes. So we always have to look out for a resting place near sunset, for should we happen to be flying up among the clouds when the sun goes down, we should be hurled to the depths below. We do not live here. There is another land just as beautiful as this, beyond the sea, but the way to it is very long and we have to cross the mighty ocean to get to it. There is not a single island on the way where we can spend the night. Only one solitary little rock rises just above the water midway. It is only just big enough for us to stand upon close together, and if there is a heavy sea the water splashes over us. Yet we thank our God for it. We stay there overnight in our human forms, and without it we could never revisit our beloved fatherland, for our flight takes two of the longest days in the year. We are permitted to visit the home of our father only once a year, and we dare stay for only eleven days. We hover over this big forest from whence we catch a glimpse of the palace where we were born, and where our father lives. Beyond it we can see the high church towers where our mother is buried. We fancy that the trees and bushes here are related to us, and the wild horses gallop over the moors as we used to see them in our childhood. The charcoal burners still sing the old songs we used to dance to when we were children. This is our fatherland. We are drawn towards it and here we have found you again, dear little sister. We may stay here two days longer, and then we must fly away again across the ocean, to a lovely country indeed, but it is not our own dear fatherland. How shall we ever take you with us? We have neither ship nor boat."

"How can I deliver you?" said their sister, and they went on talking to each other nearly all night. They only dozed for a few hours.

Elise was awakened in the morning by the rustling of the swans' wings above her. Her brothers were again transformed and were wheeling round in great circles, till she lost sight of them in the distance. One of them, the youngest, stayed behind. He laid his head against her bosom and she caressed it with her fingers. They remained together all day. Towards evening the others came back, and as soon as the sun went down they took their natural forms.

"Tomorrow we must fly away and we dare not come back for a whole year, but we can't leave you like this. Have you courage to go with us? My wings are strong enough to carry you over the forest, so our united strength ought to be sufficient to bear you across the ocean."

"Oh yes! Take me with you," said Elise.

They spent the whole night in weaving a kind of net of the elastic bark of the willow, bound together with tough rushes. They made it both large and strong. Elise lay down upon it, and when the sun rose and the brothers became swans again, they took up the net in their bills and flew high up among the clouds with their precious sister, who was fast asleep. As the sunbeams fell straight onto her face, one of the swans flew over her head so that his broad wings should shade her.

They were far from land when Elise woke. She thought she must still be dreaming—it seemed so strange to be carried through the air so high up above the sea. By her side lay a branch of beautiful ripe berries and a bundle of savory roots, which her youngest brother had collected for her and for which she gave him a grateful smile. She knew it was he who flew above her head, shading her from the sun. They were so high up that the first ship they saw looked like a gull floating on the water. A great cloud came up behind them like a mountain, and Elise saw the shadow of herself on it, and those of the eleven swans looking like giants. It was a more beautiful picture than any she had ever seen before, but as the sun rose higher, the cloud fell behind and the shadow picture disappeared.

They flew on and on all day like arrows whizzing through the air, but they went slower than usual for now they had their sister to carry. A storm came up, and night was drawing on. With terror in her heart Elise saw the sun sinking, for the solitary rock was nowhere to be seen. The swans seemed to be taking stronger strokes than ever. Alas, she was the cause of their not being able to get on faster. As soon as the sun went down they would become men, and they would be hurled into the sea and drowned. She prayed to God from the bottom of her heart, but still no rock was to be seen. Black clouds gathered and strong gusts of wind announced a storm. The clouds looked like a great threatening leaden wave, and the flashes of lightning followed each other rapidly.

The sun was now at the edge of the sea. Elise's heart quaked, when suddenly the swans shot downwards so suddenly that she thought they were falling. Then they hovered again. Half of the sun was below the horizon, and there for the first time she saw the little rock below, which

did not look bigger than the head of a seal above the water.
The sun sank very quickly. It was no bigger than a star,
but her foot touched solid earth. The sun went out like the
last sparks of a bit of burning paper. Her brothers stood arm
in arm around her, but there was only just room enough
for them. The waves beat upon the rock and washed over
them like drenching rain. The heaven shone with continuous
fire and the thunder rolled, peal upon peal. But the sister
and brothers held each other's hands and sang a psalm which
gave them comfort and courage.

The air was pure and still at dawn. As soon as the sun
rose, the swans flew off with Elise away from the islet. The
sea still ran high. It looked from where they were as if the
white foam on the dark green water were millions of swans
floating on the waves.

When the sun rose higher, Elise saw before her, half
floating in the air, great masses of ice with shining glaciers
on the heights. Midway was perched a palace, a mile in
length, with one bold colonnade built above another. Below
swayed palm trees and gorgeous blossoms as big as mill
wheels. She asked if this was the land to which she was
going, but the swans shook their heads because what she
saw was a mirage. It was the beautiful and ever-changing
palace of Fata Morgana. No mortal dared enter it. Elise
gazed at it, but as she gazed the palace, gardens, and
mountains melted away. And in their place stood twenty
proud churches with their high towers and pointed windows.
She seemed to hear the notes of the organ, but it was the
sea she heard. When she got close to the seeming churches,
they changed to a great navy sailing beneath her, but it was
only a sea mist floating over the waters.

Yes, she saw constant changes passing before her eyes,
but now she saw the real land she was bound to. Beautiful
blue mountains rose before her with their cedar woods and
palaces. Long before the sun went down, she sat among

the hills in front of a big cave covered with delicate green creepers. It looked like a piece of embroidery.

" Now we shall see what you will dream here tonight," said the youngest brother, as he showed her where she was to sleep.

" If only I might dream how I could deliver you! " she said, and this thought filled her mind entirely. She prayed earnestly to God for His help, and even in her sleep she continued her prayer. It seemed to her that she was flying up to Fata Morgana in her castle in the air. The fairy came towards her. She was charming and brilliant, and yet she was very like the old woman who gave her the berries in the wood and told her about the swans with the golden crowns.

" Your brothers can be delivered," she said. " But have you courage and endurance enough for it? The sea is indeed softer than your hands, and it molds the hardest stones, but it does not feel the pain your fingers will feel. It has no heart and does not suffer the pain and anguish you must feel. Do you see the stinging nettle I hold in my hand? Many of this kind grow round the cave where you sleep. Only these and the ones which grow in the churchyards may be used. Mark that! Those you may pluck, although they will burn and blister your hands. Crush the nettles with your feet and you will have flax, and of this you must weave eleven coats of mail with long sleeves. Throw these over the eleven wild swans and the charm is broken. But remember, from the moment you begin this work till it is finished, even if it takes years, you must not utter a word. The first word you say will fall like a murderer's dagger into the hearts of your brothers. Their lives hang on your tongue. Mark this well."

She touched her hand at the same moment. The touch was like burning fire and it woke Elise. It was bright daylight, and close to where she slept lay a nettle like those in her

dream. She fell upon her knees with thanks to God and left
the cave to begin her work.

She seized the horrid nettles with her delicate hands, and
they burnt like fire. Great blisters rose on her hands and
arms, but she suffered it willingly if only it would deliver
her beloved brothers. She crushed every nettle with her bare
feet and twisted it into green flax.

When the sun went down and the brothers came back,
they were alarmed at finding her mute. They thought it was
some new witchcraft exercised by their wicked stepmother.
But when they saw her hands, they understood that it was
for their sakes. The youngest brother wept, and wherever his
tears fell she felt no more pain and the blisters disappeared.

She spent the whole night at her work, for she could not
rest till she had delivered her dear brothers. All the following
day, while her brothers were away, she sat solitary, but
never had the time flown so fast. One coat of mail was
finished and she began the next. Then a hunting horn sounded
among the mountains. She was frightened. The sound came
nearer and she heard dogs barking. In terror she rushed into
the cave and tied the nettles she had collected and woven
into a bundle upon which she sat.

At this moment a big dog bounded forward from the
thicket, and another and another. They barked loudly and
ran backwards and forwards. In a few minutes all the
huntsmen were standing outside the cave. The handsomest
of them was the King of the country, and he stepped up to
Elise. Never had he seen so lovely a girl.

" How came you here, beautiful child? " he said.

Elise shook her head. She dared not speak. The salvation
and the lives of her brothers depended upon her silence.
She hid her hands under her apron so that the King should
not see what she suffered.

"Come with me," he said. "You cannot stay here. If you
are as good as you are beautiful, I will dress you in silks

and velvets, put a golden crown upon your head, and you shall live with me and have your home in my richest palace." Then he lifted her upon his horse. She wept and wrung her hands, but the King said, " I think only of your happiness. You will thank me one day for what I am doing." Then he darted off across the mountains, holding her before him on his horse, and the huntsmen followed.

When the sun went down, the royal city with churches and cupolas lay before them, and the King led her into the palace. Here great fountains played in the marble halls and the walls and ceilings were adorned with paintings, but she had no eyes for them. She only wept and sorrowed. Passively she allowed the women to dress her in royal robes, to twist pearls into her hair, and to draw gloves onto her blistered hands.

She was dazzlingly lovely as she stood there in all her magnificence. The courtiers bent low before her and the King wooed her as his bride, although the archbishop shook his head and whispered that he feared the beautiful wood maiden was a witch, who had dazzled their eyes and infatuated the King.

The King refused to listen to him. He ordered the music to play, the richest food to be brought, and the loveliest girls to dance before her. She was led through scented gardens into gorgeous apartments, but nothing brought a smile to her lips or into her eyes. Sorrow sat there like a heritage and a possession for all time. Last of all, the King opened the door of a little chamber close by the room where she was to sleep. It was adorned with costly green carpets and made to exactly resemble the cave where he found her. On the floor lay the bundle of flax she had spun from the nettles, and from the ceiling hung the shirt of mail which was already finished. One of the huntsmen had brought all these things away as curiosities.

"Here you may dream that you are back in your former home," said the King. "Here is the work upon which you were engaged. In the midst of your splendor it may amuse you to think of those times."

When Elise saw all these things so dear to her heart, a smile for the first time played upon her lips and the blood rushed back to her cheeks. She thought of the deliverance of her brothers and she kissed the King's hand. He pressed her to his heart and ordered all the church bells to ring marriage peals. The lovely dumb girl from the woods was to be Queen of the country.

The archbishop whispered evil words into the ear of the King, but they did not reach his heart. The wedding was to take place and the archbishop himself had to put the crown upon her head. In his anger he pressed the golden circlet so tightly upon her head that it gave her pain. But a heavier circlet pressed upon her heart, her grief for her brothers, so she thought nothing of the bodily pain. Her lips were sealed. A single word from her mouth would cost her brothers their lives, but her eyes were full of love for the good and handsome King, who did everything he could to please her.

Every day she grew more and more attached to him. She longed to confide in him and tell him her sufferings, but dumb she must remain and in silence must bring her labor to completion. Therefore at night she stole away from his side into her secret chamber, which was decorated like a cave, and here she knitted one shirt after another. When she came to the seventh, all her flax was worked up. She knew that these nettles which she was to use grew in the churchyard, but she had to pluck them herself. How was she to get there?

"Oh, what is the pain of my fingers compared with the anguish of my heart?" she thought. "I must venture out. The good God will not desert me."

With as much terror in her heart as if she were doing some evil deed, she stole down one night into the moonlit garden and through the long alleys out into the silent streets to the churchyard. It was very dark and lonely, but she picked the stinging nettles and hurried back to the palace with them. Only one person saw her but that was the archbishop, who watched while others slept. Surely now all his bad opinions of the Queen were justified. All was not as it should be with her. She must be a witch, and therefore she had bewitched the King and all the people.

He told the King in the confessional what he had seen and what he feared. When those bad words passed his lips, the pictures of the saints shook their heads as if to say, "It is not so. Elise is innocent." The archbishop, however, took it differently. He thought they were bearing witness against her and shaking their heads at her sin.

Two big tears rolled down the King's cheeks, and he went home with doubt in his heart. He pretended to sleep at night, but no quiet sleep came to his eyes. He perceived how Elise got up and went to her private closet. Day by day his face grew darker. Elise saw it but could not imagine what was the cause of it. It alarmed her, and what was she not already suffering in her heart because of her brothers? Her salt tears ran down upon the royal purple velvet and lay there like sparkling diamonds, and all who saw their splendor wished to be Queen.

She had, however, almost reached the end for her labors. Only one shirt of mail was wanting, but again she had no more flax and not a single nettle was left. Once more, for the last time, she must go to the churchyard to pluck a few handfuls. She thought with dread of the solitary walk and the darkness, but her will was as strong as her trust in God.

Elise went, but the King and the archbishop followed her. They saw her disappear within the grated gateway of the

churchyard. The King was very sorrowful, because he thought
she must surely be a witch.

"The people must judge her," he groaned. And the people
judged: "Let her be consumed in the glowing flames."

She was led from her beautiful royal apartments to a dark
damp dungeon, where the wind whistled through the grated
window. Instead of velvet and silk they gave her the bundle
of nettles she had gathered to lay her head upon. The hard
burning shirts of mail were to be her covering, but they could
have given her nothing more precious.

She set to work again with many prayers to God. Outside
her prison the street boys sang derisive songs about her,
and not a soul comforted her with a kind word.

Towards evening she heard the rustle of swans' wings
close to her window. It was her youngest brother, who at
last had found her. He sobbed aloud with joy although he
knew that the coming night might be her last. But then
her work was almost done and her brothers were there.

The archbishop came to stay with her during her last
hours, as he had promised the King. She shook her head at
him and by looks and gestures begged him to leave her.
She had only this night in which to finish her work, or else
all would be wasted—all her pain, her tears and her sleepless
nights. The archbishop went away with bitter words against
her, but poor Elise knew that she was innocent, and she
went on with her work.

The little mice ran about the floor, bringing nettles to her
feet so as to give what help they could, and a thrush sat on
the grating of the window, where he sang all night as merrily
as he could to keep up her courage.

It was still only dawn and the sun would not rise for an
hour, when the eleven brothers stood at the gate of the
palace, begging to be taken to the King. This could not be
done, they were told, for it was still night. The King was
asleep and no one dared wake him. All their entreaties and

threats were useless. The watch turned out and even the King himself came to see what was the matter. But just then the sun rose, and no more brothers were to be seen—only eleven wild swans hovering over the palace.

The whole populace streamed out of the town gates. They were all anxious to see the witch burnt. A miserable horse drew the cart in which Elise was seated. They had put upon her a smock of green sacking, and all her beautiful long hair hung loose from the lovely head. Her cheeks were deathly pale and her lips moved softly, while her fingers unceasingly twisted the green yarn. Even on the way to her death she could not abandon her unfinished work. Ten shirts lay completed at her feet. She labored away at the eleventh amid the scoffing insults of the populace.

" Look at the witch! How she mutters! She has no book of psalms in her hands. There she sits with her loathsome sorcery. Tear it away from her and into a thousand bits! "

The crowd pressed around her to destroy her work, but just then eleven wild swans flew down and perched upon the cart, flapping their wings. The crowd gave way before them in terror.

" It is a sign from Heaven! She is innocent," they whispered. But they dared not say it aloud.

The executioner seized her by the hand but she hastily threw the eleven shirts over the swans, who were immediately transformed to eleven handsome princes. But the youngest had a swan's wing in place of an arm, for one sleeve was wanting to his shirt of mail. She had not been able to finish it.

" Now I may speak! I am innocent."

The populace who saw what had happened bowed down before her as if she had been a saint, but she sank lifeless in her brother's arms. So great had been the strain, the terror, and the suffering she had endured.

" Yes, innocent she is indeed," said the eldest brother, and he told them all that had happened.

Whilst he spoke a wonderful fragrance spread around, as of millions of roses. Every faggot in the pile had taken root and shot out branches, and a great high hedge of red roses had arisen. At the very top was one pure white blossom. It shone like a star, and the King broke it off and laid it on Elise's bosom, and she woke with joy and peace in her heart.

All the church bells began to ring of their own accord, and the singing birds flocked around them. Surely such a bridal procession went back to the palace as no king had ever seen before!

Great Claus and Little Claus

In a village there once lived two men of the selfsame name. They were both called Claus, but one of them had four horses and the other had only one. So to distinguish them, people called the owner of the four horses "Great Claus," and he who had only one horse was called "Little Claus." Now I shall tell you what happened to them, for this is a true story.

Throughout the week Little Claus was obliged to plow for Great Claus and to lend him his one horse, but once a week—on Sunday—Great Claus lent him all his four horses. How proudly each Sunday Little Claus would smack his whip over all five, for they were as good as his own on that one day.

The sun shone brightly and the church bells rang merrily as the people passed by, dressed in their best and with their prayer books under their arms. They were going to hear the parson preach. They looked at Little Claus plowing with his five horses, and he was so proud that he smacked his whip and said, "Gee-up, my five horses."

"You mustn't say that," said Great Claus, "for only one of them is yours."

But Little Claus soon forgot what he ought not to say, and when anyone passed he would call out, "Gee-up, my five horses."

"I must really beg you not to say that again," said Great
Claus. "If you do, I shall hit your horse on the head so
that he will drop down dead on the spot. And that will be
the end of him."

"I promise you I will not say it again," said the other.
But as soon as anybody came by nodding to him and wishing
him "Good day," he was so pleased and thought how grand
it was to have five horses plowing in his field that he cried
out again, "Gee-up, all my horses!"

"I'll gee-up your horses for you," said Great Claus. And
seizing the tethering mallet he struck Little Claus's one horse
on the head, and it fell down dead.

"Oh, now I have no horse at all," said Little Claus,
weeping. But after a while he flayed the dead horse and
hung the skin in the wind to dry.

Then he put the dried skin into a bag, hung it over his
shoulder, and went off to the next town to sell it. But he
had a long way to go and had to pass through a dark and
gloomy forest.

Presently a storm arose and he lost his way. And before
he discovered the right path, evening was drawing on, and
it was still a long way to the town and too far to return
home before nightfall.

Near the road stood a large farmhouse. The shutters
outside the windows were closed, but lights shone through
the crevices and at the top. "They might let me stay here
for the night," thought Little Claus, so he went up to the
door and knocked.

The farmer's wife opened the door, but when she heard
what he wanted she told him to go away. Her husband was
not at home and she could not let any strangers in.

"Then I shall have to lie out here," said Little Claus to
himself, as the farmer's wife shut the door in his face.

Close to the farmhouse stood a large haystack, and
between it and the house there was a small shed with a

thatched roof. "I can lie up there," said Little Claus, as he saw the roof. "It will make a famous bed, but I hope the stork won't fly down and bite my legs." A live stork who had his nest on the roof was standing up there.

So Little Claus climbed on to the roof of the shed. And as he turned about to make himself comfortable, he discovered that the wooden shutters did not reach to the top of the windows. He could see into the room, in which a large table was laid out with wine, roast meat, and a splendid fish. The farmer's wife and the sexton were sitting at table together. Nobody else was there. She was filling his glass and helping him plentifully to fish, which appeared to be his favorite dish.

"If only I could have some too," thought Little Claus. Then he stretched out his neck towards the window and spied a beautiful large cake. Indeed, they had a glorious feast before them.

At that moment he heard someone riding down the road towards the farm. It was the farmer coming home.

He was a good man but he had one very strange prejudice—he could not bear the sight of a sexton. If he happened to see one, he would get into a terrible rage. Because of this dislike, the sexton had gone to visit the farmer's wife during her husband's absence from home, and the good woman had put before him the best of everything she had in the house to eat.

When they heard the farmer they were dreadfully frightened, and the woman made the sexton creep into a large chest which stood in a corner. He went at once, for he was well aware of the poor man's aversion to the sight of a sexton. The woman then quickly hid all the nice things and the wine in the oven, because if her husband had seen it he would have asked why it was provided.

"Oh dear," sighed Little Claus, on the roof, when he saw the food disappearing.

"Is there anyone up there?" asked the farmer, peering up at Little Claus. "What are you doing up there? You had better come into the house."

Then Little Claus told him how he had lost his way and asked if he might have shelter for the night.

"Certainly," said the farmer. "But the first thing is to have something to eat."

The woman received them both very kindly, laid the table, and gave them a large bowl of porridge. The farmer was hungry and ate it with a good appetite, but Little Claus could not help thinking of the good roast meat, the fish, and the cake, which he knew were hidden in the oven. He had put his sack with the hide in it under the table by his feet, for as we remember he was on his way to the town to sell it. He did not fancy the porridge, so he trod on the sack and made the dried hide squeak quite loudly.

"Hush!" said Little Claus to his sack, at the same time treading on it again so that it squeaked louder than ever.

"What on earth have you got in your sack?" asked the farmer.

"Oh, it's a goblin," said Little Claus. "He says we needn't eat the porridge, for he has charmed the oven full of roast meat and fish and cake."

"What do you say?" said the farmer, opening the oven door with all speed and seeing the nice things the woman had hidden, but which her husband thought the goblin had produced for their special benefit.

The woman dared not say anything but put the food before them, and then they both made a hearty meal of the fish, the meat, and the cake.

Then Little Claus trod on the skin and made it squeak again.

"What does he say now?" asked the farmer.

"He says," answered Little Claus, "that he has also charmed three bottles of wine into the oven for us."

So the woman had to bring out the wine too, and the farmer drank it and became very merry. Wouldn't he like to have a goblin for himself, like the one in Little Claus's sack!

"Can he charm out the devil?" asked the farmer. "I shouldn't mind seeing him, now that I am in such a merry mood."

"Oh yes!" said Little Claus. "My goblin can do everything that we ask him. Can't you?" he asked, trampling on the sack till it squeaked louder than ever. "Did you hear him say yes? But the devil is so ugly, you'd better not see him."

"Oh, I'm not a bit frightened. Whatever does he look like?"

"Well, he will show himself in the image of a sexton."

"Oh dear!" said the farmer. "That's bad! I must tell you that I can't bear to see a sexton. However, it doesn't matter. I shall know it's only the devil and then I shan't mind so much. Now my courage is up! But he mustn't come too close."

"I'll ask my goblin about it," said Little Claus, treading on the bag and putting his ear close to it.

"What does he say?"

"He says you can go along and open the chest in the corner, and there you'll see the devil moping in the dark. But hold the lid tight so that he doesn't get out."

"Will you help me to hold it?" asked the farmer, going along to the chest where the woman had hidden the real sexton, who was shivering with fright. The farmer lifted up the lid a wee little bit and peeped in.

"Ha!" he shrieked, and sprang back. "Yes, I saw him and he looked just exactly like our sexton. It was a horrible sight!" They had to have a drink after this, and there they sat drinking till far into the night.

"You must sell me that goblin," said the farmer. "You

may ask what you like for him! I'll give you a bushel of
money for him."

"No, I can't do that," said Little Claus. "You must remember how useful my goblin is to me."

"Oh, but I should so like to have him," said the farmer
and he went on begging for him.

"Well," said Little Claus at last, "as you have been so
kind to me I shall have to give him up. You shall have him
for a bushel of money, but I must have it full to the brim."

"You shall have it," said the farmer. "But you must take
that chest away with you! I won't have it in the house for
another hour. I'd never know whether he's there or not."

So Little Claus gave his sack with the dried hide in it to
the farmer and received in return a bushel of money, and the
measure was full to the brim. The farmer also gave him a
large wheelbarrow to take the money and the chest away in.

"Good-bye," said Little Claus, and off he went with his
money and the big chest with the sexton in it.

There was a wide and deep river on the other side of the
wood. The current was so strong that it was almost impossible to swim against it. A large new bridge had been
built across it, and when they got into the very middle of
it, Little Claus said quite loud, so that the sexton could
hear him, "What am I to do with this stupid old chest? It
might be full of paving stones—it's so heavy. I am quite
tired of wheeling it along, so I'll just throw it into the river.
If it floats down the river to my house, well and good; and
if it doesn't, I shan't care."

Then he took hold of the chest and raised it up a bit,
as if he were about to throw it into the river.

"No, no! Let it be!" shouted the sexton. "Let me get
out!"

"Hullo!" said Little Claus, pretending to be frightened.
"Why, he's still inside it! Then I must heave it into the
river to drown him."

"Oh no! Oh no!" shouted the sexton. "I'll give you a bushel full of money if you'll let me out!"

"Oh, that's another matter," said Little Claus, opening the chest. The sexton crept out at once and pushed the empty chest into the water, and then went home and gave Little Claus a whole bushel full of money. He had already had one from the farmer, you know, so now his wheelbarrow was quite full of money.

"I got a pretty fair price for that horse, I must admit," said he to himself when he got home to his own room and turned the money out of the wheelbarrow into a heap on the floor. "What a rage Great Claus will be in when he discovers how rich I have become through my one horse. But I won't tell him the truth about it." So he sent a boy to Great Claus to borrow a bushel measure.

"What does he want that for?" thought Great Claus. And he rubbed some tallow on the bottom of the measure, so that a little of whatever was to be measured might stick to it. So it did, for when the measure came back three new silver threepenny bits were sticking to it.

"What's this?" said Great Claus, and he ran straight along to Little Claus. "Where on earth did you get all that money?"

"Oh, that was for my horse's hide which I sold last night."

"That was well paid, indeed!" said Great Claus. And he ran home, took an ax, and hit all his four horses on the head. He then flayed them and went off to the town with the hides.

"Skins! Skins! Who will buy skins?" he shouted up and down the streets.

All the shoemakers and tanners in the town came running up and asked him how much he wanted for them.

"A bushel of money for each," said Great Claus.

"Are you mad?" they all said. "Do you imagine we have money by the bushel?"

"Skins! Skins! Who will buy skins?" he shouted again.

The shoemakers took up their measures and the tanners their leather aprons, and beat Great Claus through the town. "Skins! Skins!" they mocked him. "Yes, we'll give you a raw hide. Out the town with him!" they shouted, and Great Claus had to hurry off as fast as ever he could go. He had never had such a beating in his life.

"Little Claus shall pay for this," he said when he got home. "I'll kill him for it."

Little Claus's old grandmother had just died in his house. She certainly had been very cross and unkind to him, but now that she was dead he felt quite sorry about it. He took the dead woman and put her into his warm bed to see if he could bring her to life again. He meant her to stay there all night, and he would sit on a chair in the corner. He had slept like that before.

As he sat there in the night, the door opened and in came Great Claus with his ax. He knew where Little Claus's bed stood, and he went straight up to it and hit the dead grandmother a blow on the forehead, thinking that it was Little Claus.

"Just see if you'll cheat me again after that," he said. Then he went home again.

"What a bad, wicked man he is," said Little Claus. "He was going to kill me there. What a good thing that poor old granny was dead already, or else he would have killed her."

He now dressed his old grandmother in her best Sunday clothes, borrowed a horse from his neighbor, harnessed it to a cart, and set his grandmother on the back seat so that she could not fall out when the cart moved. Then he started off through the wood. When the sun rose he was just outside a big inn, and Little Claus drew up his horse and went in to get something to eat. The landlord was a very, very rich man and a very good man, but he was fiery-tempered, as if he were made of pepper and tobacco.

" Good morning," said he to Little Claus. " You've got your
best clothes on very early this morning! "

" Yes," said Little Claus. " I'm going to town with my old
grandmother. She's sitting out there in the cart. I can't get
her to come in. Won't you take her out a glass of mead?
You'll have to shout at her, for she's very hard of hearing."

" Yes, she shall have it," said the innkeeper, and he poured
out a large glass of mead which he took out to the dead
grandmother in the cart.

" Here is a glass of mead your son has sent," said the
innkeeper, but the dead woman sat quite still and never
said a word. " Don't you hear? " shouted the innkeeper as
loud as he could. " Here is a glass of mead from your son! "

Again he shouted and then again as loud as ever, but
as she did not stir he got angry and threw the glass of
mead in her face. The mead ran all over her and she fell
backwards out of the cart, for she was only stuck up and
not tied in.

" Now," shouted Little Claus, as he rushed out of the
inn and seized the landlord by the neck. " You have killed
my grandmother! Just look! There's a great hole in her
forehead."

" Oh, what a misfortune! " exclaimed the innkeeper,
clasping his hands. " That's the consequence of my fiery
temper. Good Little Claus, I will give you a bushel of
money and bury your grandmother as if she had been my
own, if you will only say nothing about it. Otherwise they
will chop my head off, and that is so nasty."

So Little Claus had a whole bushel of money, and the
innkeeper buried the old grandmother just as if she had been
his own.

When Little Claus got home again with his money, he
immediately sent his boy over to Great Claus to borrow his
measure.

" What? " said Great Claus, " Is he not dead? I shall have

to go and see about it myself." So he took the measure over
to Little Claus himself.

"I say, wherever did you get all that money?" asked he,
his eyes round with amazement at what he saw.

"It was my grandmother you killed instead of me," said
Little Claus. "I have sold her and got a bushel of money
for her."

"That was good pay indeed!" said Great Claus, so he
hurried home, took an ax, and killed his old grandmother.

He then put her in a cart and drove off to town with
her where the apothecary lived, and asked if he would buy
a dead body.

"Who is it, and where did the body come from?" asked
the apothecary.

"It is my grandmother, and I have killed her for a bushel
of money," said Great Claus.

"Heaven preserve us!" said the apothecary. "You are
talking like a madman. Pray don't say such things! You
might lose your head." And he pointed out to him what a
horribly wicked thing he had done and what a bad man he
was, and that he deserved to be punished. Great Claus was
so frightened that he rushed straight out of the shop, jumped
into the cart, whipped up his horse, and galloped home.
The apothecary and everyone else thought he was mad, and
so they let him drive off.

"You shall be paid for this!" said Great Claus, when he
got out on the highroad. "You shall pay for this, Little
Claus!"

As soon as he got home, he took the biggest sack he could
find, went over to Little Claus and said, "You have deceived
me again. First I killed my horses, and then my old grandmother. It's all your fault, but you shan't have the chance of
cheating me again!" Then he took Little Claus by the waist
and put him into the sack, put it on his back, and shouted
to him, "I'm going to drown you now!"

It was a long way to go before he came to the river, and Little Claus was not so light to carry. The road passed close by a church in which the organ was playing, and the people were singing beautifully. Great Claus put down the sack with Little Claus in it close by the church door. He thought he would like to go and hear a psalm before he went any further. As Little Claus could not get out of the bag, and all the people were in the church, Great Claus went in too.

" Oh dear, oh dear! " sighed Little Claus in the sack. He turned and twisted, but it was impossible to undo the cord. Just then an old cattle drover with white hair and a tall stick in his hand came along. He had a whole drove of cows and bulls before him. They ran against the sack Little Claus was in and upset it.

" Oh dear," sighed Little Claus. "I am so young to be going to the Kingdom of Heaven! "

" And I," said the cattle drover, " am so old and cannot get there yet! "

" Open the sack! " shouted Little Claus. " Get in in place of me, and you will get to Heaven directly."

" That will just suit me," said the cattle drover, undoing the sack for Little Claus, who immediately sprang out. " You must look after the cattle now," said the old man as he crept into the sack. Little Claus tied it up and walked off driving the cattle before him.

A little while afterwards Great Claus came out of the church. He took the sack again on his back and he certainly thought it had grown lighter, for the old cattle drover was not more than half the weight of Little Claus.

" How light he seems to have got! That must be because I have been to church and said my prayers." Then he went on to the river, which was both wide and deep, and threw the sack with the old cattle drover in it into the water.

" Now, you won't cheat me again! " he shouted, for he thought it was Little Claus.

Then he went homewards, but when he reached the cross-roads he met Little Claus with his herd of cattle.

"What's the meaning of this?" exclaimed Great Claus. "Didn't I drown you?"

"Yes," said Little Claus. "It's just about half an hour since you threw me into the river."

"But where did you get all those splendid beasts?" asked Great Claus.

"They are sea cattle," said Little Claus. "I will tell you the whole story, and indeed I thank you heartily for drowning me. I'm at the top of the tree now and a very rich man, I can tell you. I was so frightened when I was in the sack! The wind whistled in my ears when you threw me over the bridge into the cold water. I immediately sank to the bottom but I was not hurt, for the grass is beautifully soft down there. The sack was opened at once by a beautiful maiden in snow-white clothes with a green wreath on her wet hair. She took my hand and said, 'Are you there, Little Claus? Here are some cattle for you, and a mile further up the road you will come upon another herd which I will give you too!' Then I saw that the river was a great highway for the sea folk. Down at the bottom of it they walked and drove about, from the sea right up to the end of the river. The flowers were lovely and the grass was so fresh! The fishes which swam about glided close to me just like birds in the air. How nice the people were, and what a lot of cattle strolled about in the ditches!"

"But why did you come straight up here again then?" asked Great Claus. "I shouldn't have done that if it was so fine down there."

"Oh," said Little Claus, "that's just my cunning. You remember I told you the mermaid said that a mile further up the road—and by the road she means the river, for she can't go anywhere else—I should find another herd of cattle waiting for me. Well, I know how many bends there are in the river and what a roundabout way it would be. It's ever so much shorter if you can come up on dry land and take the short cuts. You save a couple of miles by it and can get the cattle much sooner."

"Oh, you *are* a fortunate man," said Great Claus. "Do you think I should get some sea cattle if I were to go down to the bottom of the river?"

"I'm sure you would," said Little Claus. "But I can't carry you in the sack to the river. You're too heavy for me. If you'd like to walk there and then get into the sack, I'll throw you into the river with the greatest pleasure in the world."

"Thank you," said Great Claus. "But if I don't get any sea cattle when I get down there, see if I don't give you a sound thrashing."

"Oh, don't be so hard on me!" said Little Claus.

Then they walked off to the river. As soon as the cattle saw the water they rushed down to drink, for they were very thirsty. "See what a hurry they're in," said Little Claus. "They want to get down to the bottom again."

"Now, help me first," said Great Claus, "or else I'll thrash you." He then crept into a big sack which had been lying across the back of one of the cows. "Put a big stone in, or I'm afraid I shan't sink," said Great Claus.

"Oh, have no fear of that," said Little Claus, and he put a big stone into the sack and gave it a push. Plump went the sack and Great Claus was in the river, where he sank to the bottom at once.

"I'm afraid he won't find any cattle," said Little Claus, as he drove his herd home.

The Steadfast Tin Soldier

There were once five and twenty tin soldiers, all brothers, for they were the offspring of the same old tin spoon. Each man shouldered his gun, kept his eyes well to the front, and wore the smartest red and blue uniform imaginable. The first thing they heard in their new world, when the lid was taken off the box, was a little boy clapping his hands and crying, " Soldiers, soldiers! "

It was his birthday and they had just been given to him, so he lost no time in setting them up on the table. All the soldiers were exactly alike with one exception, and he differed from the rest in having only one leg. For he was made last, and there was not quite enough tin left to finish him. However, he stood just as well on his one leg as the others did on two. In fact he was the very one who became famous.

On the table where they were being set up were many other toys, but the chief thing which caught the eye was a delightful paper castle. You could see through the tiny windows right into the rooms. Outside there were some little trees surrounding a small mirror, representing a lake, whose surface reflected the waxen swans which were swimming about on it. It was altogether charming, but the prettiest thing of all was a little maiden standing at the open door of the castle.

She too was cut out of paper, but she wore a dress of the

lightest gauze, with a dainty little blue ribbon over her shoulders, by way of a scarf, set off by a brilliant spangle as big as her whole face. The little maid was stretching out both arms, for she was a dancer. And in the dance one of her legs was raised so high into the air that the tin soldier could see absolutely nothing of it, and supposed that she like himself had but one leg.

"That would be the very wife for me!" he thought, "but she is much too grand. She lives in a palace, while I only have a box, and then there are five and twenty of us to share it. No, that would be no place for her. But I must try to make her acquaintance!" Then he lay down full length behind a snuffbox which stood on the table. From that point he could have a good look at the lady, who continued to stand on one leg without losing her balance.

Late in the evening the other soldiers were put into their box, and the people of the house went to bed. Now was the time for the toys to play. They amused themselves with paying visits, fighting battles, and giving balls. The tin soldiers rustled about in their box for they wanted to join the games, but they could not get the lid off. The nutcrackers turned somersaults and the pencil scribbled nonsense on the slate. There was such a noise that the canary woke up and joined in, but his remarks were in verse. The only two who did not move were the tin soldier and the little dancer. She stood as stiff as ever on tiptoe, with her arms spread out. He was equally firm on his one leg, and he did not take his eyes off her for a moment.

Then the clock struck twelve, when pop! up flew the lid of the snuffbox, but there was no snuff in it. No! There was a little black goblin, a sort of jack-in-the-box.

"Tin soldier," said the goblin, "have the goodness to keep your eyes to yourself." But the tin soldier feigned not to hear.

"Ah! you just wait till tomorrow," said the goblin.

In the morning when the children got up, they put the

tin soldier on the window frame, and whether it was caused
by the goblin or by a puff of wind, I do not know, but all
at once the window burst open and the soldier fell head
foremost from the third story.

It was a terrific descent, and he landed at last with his
leg in the air and resting on his cap, with his bayonet fixed
between two paving stones. The maidservant and the little
boy ran down at once to look for him, but although they
almost trod on him they could not see him. Had the soldier
called out, "Here I am!" they would have found him. But
he did not think it proper to shout when he was in uniform.

Presently it began to rain, and the drops fell faster and
faster till there was a regular torrent. When it was over, two
street boys came along. "Look out!" said one. "There is a
tin soldier. He shall go for a sail."

So they made a boat out of a newspaper and put the soldier
into the middle of it, and he sailed away down the gutter.
Both boys ran alongside clapping their hands. Good heavens!
what waves there were in the gutter, and what a current,
but then it certainly had rained cats and dogs. The paper
boat danced up and down, and now and then whirled round
and round. A shudder ran through the tin soldier, but he
remained undaunted and did not move a muscle. He only
looked straight before him with his gun shouldered. All at
once the boat drifted under a long wooden tunnel, and it
became as dark as it was in his box.

"Where on earth am I going now?" thought he. "Well,
well, it is all the fault of that goblin! Oh, if only the little
maiden were with me in the boat, it might be twice as dark
for all I should care."

At this moment a big water rat, who lived in the tunnel,
came up.

"Have you a pass?" asked the rat. "Hand up your pass."

The tin soldier did not speak, but clung still tighter to his
gun. The boat rushed on, the rat close behind. Phew, how

he gnashed his teeth and shouted to the bits of stick and straw, "Stop him! Stop him! He hasn't paid his toll. He hasn't shown his pass."

But the current grew stronger and stronger. The tin soldier could already see daylight before him at the end of the tunnel, but he also heard a roaring sound, fit to strike terror to the bravest heart. Just imagine: where the tunnel ended, the stream rushed straight into the big canal. That would be just as dangerous for him as it would be for us to shoot a great rapid.

He was so near the end now that it was impossible to stop. The boat dashed out. The poor tin soldier held himself as stiff as he could. No one should say of him that he even winced!

The boat swirled round three or four times and filled with water to the edge; it must sink. The tin soldier stood up to his neck in water, and the boat sank deeper and deeper. The paper became limper and limper, and at last the water went over his head. Then he thought of the pretty little dancer whom he was never to see again, and this refrain rang in his ears:

> "*Onward! Onward! Soldier!*
> *For death thou canst not shun.*"

At last the paper gave way entirely and the soldier fell through, but at the same moment he was swallowed by a big fish.

Oh, how dark it was inside the fish! It was worse even than being in the tunnel. And then it was so narrow! But the tin soldier was as dauntless as ever and lay full length, shouldering his gun.

The fish rushed about and made the most frantic movements. At last it became quite quiet, and after a time a flash like lightning pierced it. The soldier was once more in the broad daylight, and someone called out loudly, "A tin soldier!" The fish had been caught, taken to market, sold,

Suddenly the tin soldier was about to be swallowed by a great fish!

and brought into the kitchen, where the cook cut it open with a large knife. She took the soldier up by the waist with two fingers and carried him into the parlor, where everyone wanted to see the wonderful man who had traveled about in the stomach of a fish. But the tin soldier was not at all proud. They set him up on the table, and—wonder of wonders! he found himself in the very same room that he had been in before. He saw the very same children, and the toys were still standing on the table, as well as the beautiful castle with the pretty little dancer.

She still stood on one leg and held the other up in the air. You see, she also was unbending. The soldier was so much moved that he was ready to shed tears of tin, but that would not have been fitting. He looked at her and she looked at him, but they said never a word. At this moment one of the little boys took up the tin soldier, and without rhyme or reason threw him into the fire. No doubt the little goblin in the snuffbox was to blame for that. The tin soldier stood there, lighted up by the flame and in the most horrible heat, but whether it was the heat of the real fire, or the warmth of his feelings, he did not know. He had lost all his gay color. It might have been from his perilous journey, or it might have been from grief. Who can tell?

He looked at the little maiden and she looked at him, and he felt that he was melting away, but he still managed to keep himself erect, shouldering his gun bravely.

A door was suddenly opened. The draught caught the little dancer and she fluttered like a sylph, straight into the fire, to the soldier, blazed up and was gone!

By this time the soldier was reduced to a mere lump, and when the maid took away the ashes next morning she found him in the shape of a small tin heart. All that was left of the dancer was her spangle, and that was burned as black as a coal.

Ole Shut-Eye

In the whole world there is nobody who knows so many stories as Ole Shut-Eye; he can tell capital ones!

As evening comes on, when the children still sit nicely at table or on their stools, then comes Ole Shut-Eye. He comes up the stairs quite softly, for he walks in his stocking feet; he opens the door noiselessly, and st! he squirts sweet milk in the children's eyes, a small, small stream, but enough to prevent them from keeping their eyes open; and thus they cannot see him. He creeps just among them, and blows softly upon their necks, and this makes their heads heavy. O yes, but it doesn't hurt them, for Ole Shut-Eye is very fond of the children; he only wants them to be quiet, and that they are not until they are taken to bed: they are to be quiet that he may tell them stories.

When the children sleep, Ole Shut-Eye sits down upon their bed. He is well dressed: his coat is of silk, but it is impossible to say of what color, for it shines red, green, and blue, according as he turns. Under each arm he carries an umbrella: the one with pictures on it he spreads over the good children, and then they dream all night the most glorious stories; but on his other umbrella nothing at all is painted, and this he spreads over the naughty children, and these sleep in a dull way, and when they awake in the morning they have not dreamed of anything.

Now we shall hear how Ole Shut-Eye, every evening through one whole week, came to a little boy named Hjalmar, and what he told him. There are seven stories, for there are seven days in the week.

"Listen," said Ole Shut-Eye in the evening, when he had put Hjalmar to bed; "now I'll clear up."

And all the flowers in the flowerpots became great trees, stretching out their long branches under the ceiling of the room and along the walls, so that the whole room looked like a lovely bower; and all the twigs were covered with flowers, and each flower was more beautiful than a rose, and smelt so sweet that one wanted to eat it; it was sweeter than jam. The fruit gleamed like gold, and there were cakes bursting with raisins. It was splendid. But at the same time a terrible wail sounded from the table drawer, where Hjalmar's schoolbook lay.

"Whatever can that be?" said Ole Shut-Eye; and he went to the table, and opened the drawer. It was the slate which was suffering from convulsions, for a wrong number had got into the sum, so that it was nearly falling in pieces; the slate pencil tugged and jumped at its string, as if it had been a little dog who wanted to help the sum; but he could not. And thus there was a great lamentation in Hjalmar's copybook; it was quite terrible to hear. On each page the great letters stood in a row, one underneath the other, and each with a little one at its side; that was the copy; and next to these were a few more letters which thought they looked just like the first; and these Hjalmar had written; but they lay down just as if they had tumbled over the pencil lines on which they were to stand.

"See, this is how you should hold yourselves," said the Copy. "Look, sloping in this way, with a powerful swing!"

"O, we should be very glad to do that," replied Hjalmar's Letters, "but we cannot; we are too weakly."

"Then you must take medicine," said Ole Shut-Eye.

"O no," cried they; and they immediately stood up so gracefully that it was beautiful to behold.

"Yes, now we cannot tell any stories," said Ole Shut-Eye; "now I must exercise them. One, two; one, two!" and thus he exercised the Letters; and they stood quite slender, and as beautiful as any copy can be. But when Ole Shut-Eye went away, and Hjalmar looked at them next morning, they were as weak and miserable as ever.

TUESDAY

As soon as Hjalmar was in bed, Ole Shut-Eye touched all the articles of furniture in the room with his little magic gun, and they immediately began to talk together, and each one spoke of itself, with the exception of the spittoon, which stood silent, and was vexed that they should be so vain as to speak only of themselves, and think only of themselves, without any regard for him who stood so modestly in the corner for every one's use.

Over the chest of drawers hung a great picture in a gilt frame—it was a landscape. One saw therein large old trees, flowers in the grass, and a broad river which flowed round about a forest, past many castles, and far out into the wide ocean.

Ole Shut-Eye touched the painting with his magic gun, and the birds began to sing, the branches of the trees stirred, and the clouds began to move across it; one could see their shadows glide over the landscape.

Now Ole Shut-Eye lifted little Hjalmar up to the frame,

and put the boy's feet into the picture, just in the high grass; and there he stood; and the sun shone upon him through the branches of the trees. He ran to the water, and seated himself in a little boat which lay there; it was painted red and white, the sails gleamed like silver, and six swans, each with a gold circlet round its neck, and a bright blue star on its forehead, drew the boat past the great wood, where the trees tell of robbers and witches, and the flowers tell of the graceful little elves, and of what the butterflies have told them.

Gorgeous fishes, with scales like silver and gold, swam after their boat; sometimes they gave a spring, so that it splashed in the water; and birds, blue and red, little and great, flew after them in two long rows; the gnats danced, and the cockchafers said, "Boom! boom! " They all wanted to follow Hjalmar, and each one had a story to tell.

That was a pleasure voyage. Sometimes the forest was thick and dark, sometimes like a glorious garden full of sunlight and flowers; and there were great palaces of glass and of marble; on the balconies stood princesses, and these were all little girls whom Hjalmar knew well; he had already played with them. Each one stretched forth her hand, and held out the prettiest sugar heart which ever a cake-woman could sell; and Hjalmar took hold of each sugar heart as he passed by, and the Princess held fast, so that each of them got a piece—she the smaller share, and Hjalmar the larger. At each palace little princes stood sentry. They shouldered golden swords, and caused raisins and tin soldiers to shower down: one could see that they were real princes. Sometimes Hjalmar sailed through forests, sometimes through great halls, or through the midst of a town. He also came to the town where his nurse lived, who had carried him in her arms when he was quite a little boy, and who had always been so kind to him; and she nodded and beckoned, and

sang the pretty verse she had made herself and had sent
to Hjalmar—

> *I think of you, so oft, so oft,*
> *My own Hjalmar, ever dear;*
> *I've kissed your little lips so soft,*
> *Your forehead and your cheeks so clear.*
> *I heard you utter your first word,*
> *Then was I forced to say farewell;*
> *Now will I trust you to our Lord,*
> *A good boy here, an angel there to dwell.*

And all the birds sang too, the flowers danced on their
stalks, and the old trees nodded, just as if Ole Shut-Eye had
been telling stories to *them.*

WEDNESDAY

How the rain was streaming down without! Hjalmar could
hear it in his sleep; and when Ole Shut-Eye opened a window,
the water stood quite up to the window sill: there was
quite a lake outside, and a noble ship lay close by the house.

"If thou wilt sail with me, little Hjalmar," said Ole Shut-
Eye, "thou canst voyage tonight to foreign climes, and be
back again tomorrow."

And Hjalmar suddenly stood in his Sunday clothes upon
the glorious ship, and immediately the weather became fine,
and they sailed through the streets and steered round by the
church; and now everything was one great wild ocean. They
sailed on until land was no longer to be seen, and they saw
a number of storks, who also came from their home, and
were traveling towards the hot countries: these storks flew
in a row, one behind the other, and they had already flown
far—far! one of them was so weary that his wings would
scarcely carry him farther: he was the very last in the row,
and soon remained a great way behind the rest; at last he

sank, with outspread wings, deeper and deeper; he gave a few more strokes with his pinions, but it was of no use; now he touched the rigging of the ship with his feet, then he glided down from the sail, and—bump!—he stood upon the deck.

Now the cabin boy took him and put him into the hen coop with the fowls, ducks, and the turkeys; and the poor stork stood among them quite embarrassed.

"Just look at the fellow!" said all the fowls.

And the turkey cock swelled himself up as much as ever he could, and asked the stork who he was; and the ducks walked backward and quacked to each other, "Quackery! quackery!"

And the stork told them of hot Africa, of the pyramids, and of the ostrich, which runs like a wild horse through the desert; but the ducks did not understand what he said, and they said to one another—

"We're all of the same opinion, namely, that he's stupid."

"Yes, certainly he's stupid," said the turkey cock; and he gobbled.

Then the stork was quite silent, and thought of his Africa.

"Those are wonderful thin legs of yours," said the turkey cock. "Pray, how much do they cost a yard?"

"Quack! quack! quack!" grinned all the ducks; but the stork pretended not to hear it at all.

"You may just as well laugh too," said the turkey cock to him, "for that was very wittily said. Or was it, perhaps, too high for you? Yes, yes, he isn't very penetrating. Let us continue to be interesting among ourselves."

And then he gobbled, and the ducks quacked, "Gick! gack! gick! gack!" It was terrible how they made fun among themselves.

But Hjalmar went to the hen coop, opened the back door, and called to the stork; and the stork hopped out to him on to the deck. Now he had rested, and it seemed as if he nodded to Hjalmar, to thank him; then he spead his wings, and flew away to the warm countries; but the fowls clucked, and the ducks quacked, and the turkey cock became fiery red in the face.

"Tomorrow we shall make songs of you," said Hjalmar; and so saying he awoke, and was lying in his linen bed. It was a wonderful journey that Ole Shut-Eye had caused him to take that night.

THURSDAY

"I tell you what," said Ole Shut-Eye, "you must not be frightened. Here you shall see a little mouse," and he held out his hand with the pretty little creature in it. "It has come to invite you to a wedding. There are two little mice here who are going to enter into the marriage state tonight. They live under the floor of your mother's store closet: that is said to be a charming dwelling place!"

"But how can I get through the little mouse-hole in the ffoor?" asked Hjalmar.

"Let me manage that," said Ole Shut-Eye. "I will make you small."

And he touched Hjalmar with his magic gun, and the boy began to shrink and shrink, until he was not so long as a finger.

"Now you may borrow the uniform of a tin soldier: I think it would fit you, and it looks well to wear a uniform when one is in society."

"Yes, certainly," said Hjalmar.

And in a moment he was dressed like the smartest of tin soldiers.

"Will your honor not be kind enough to take a seat in your mamma's thimble?" asked the mouse. "Then I shall have the honor of drawing you."

" Will the young lady really take so much trouble? " cried Hjalmar.

And thus they drove to the mouse's wedding. First they came into a long passage beneath the boards, which was only just so high that they could drive through it in the thimble; and the whole passage was lit up with rotten wood.

" Is there not a delicious smell here? " observed the mouse. "The entire road has been greased with bacon rinds, and there can be nothing more exquisite."

Now they came into the festive hall. On the right hand stood all the little lady mice; and they whispered and giggled as if they were making fun of each other; on the left stood all the gentlemen mice, stroking their whiskers with their fore paws; and in the center of the hall the bridegroom and bride might be seen standing in a hollow cheese rind, and kissing each other terribly before all the guests; for this was the betrothal, and the marriage was to follow immediately.

More and more strangers kept flocking in. One mouse nearly trod another to death; and the happy couple had stationed themselves just in the doorway, so that one could neither come in nor go out. Like the passage, the room had been greased with bacon rinds, and that was the entire banquet; but for the dessert a pea was produced, in which a mouse belonging to the family had bitten the name of the betrothed pair—that is to say, the first letter of the name: that was something quite out of the common way.

All the mice said it was a beautiful wedding, and that the entertainment had been very agreeable. And then Hjalmar drove home again: he had really been in grand company; but he had been obliged to crawl, to make himself little, and to put on a tin soldier's uniform.

"It is wonderful how many grown-up people there are who would be glad to have me!" said Ole Shut-Eye; "especially those who have done something wrong. 'Good little Ole,' they say to me, 'we cannot close our eyes, and so we lie all night and see our evil deeds, which sit on the bedstead like ugly little goblins, and throw hot water over us; will you not come and drive them away, so that we may have a good sleep?' and then they sigh deeply—'We would really be glad to pay for it. Good-night, Ole: the money lies on the window sill.' But I do nothing for money," said Ole Shut-Eye.

"What shall we do this evening?" asked Hjalmar.

"I don't know if you care to go to another wedding tonight. It is of a different kind from that of yesterday. Your sister's great doll, that looks like a man, and is called Hermann, is going to marry the doll Bertha. Moreover, it is the doll's birthday, and therefore they will receive very many presents."

"Yes, I know that," replied Hjalmar. "Whenever the dolls want new clothes, my sister lets them either keep their birthday or celebrate a wedding; that has certainly happened a hundred times already."

"Yes, but tonight is the hundred and first wedding; and when number one hundred and one is past, it is all over; and that is why it will be so splendid. Only look!"

And Hjalmar looked at the table. There stood the little cardboard house with the windows illuminated, and in front of it all the tin soldiers were presenting arms. The bride and bridegroom sat quite thoughtful, and with good reason, on the floor, leaning against a leg of the table. And Ole Shut-Eye, dressed up in the grandmother's black gown, married them to each other. When the ceremony was over, all the pieces of furniture struck up the following beautiful song, which the

Pencil had written for them. It was sung to the melody of the soldiers' tattoo—

> *Let the song swell like the rushing wind,*
> *In honor of those who this day are joined,*
> *Although they stand here stiff and blind,*
> *Because they are both of a leathery kind.*
> *Hurrah! hurrah! though they're deaf and blind,*
> *Let the song swell like the rushing wind.*

And now they received presents—but they had declined to accept provisions of any kind, for they intended to live on love.

"Shall we now go into a summer lodging, or start on a journey?" asked the bridegroom.

And the swallow, who was a great traveler, and the old yard Hen, who had brought up five broods of chickens, were consulted on the subject. And the swallow told of the beautiful warm climes, where the grapes hung in ripe, heavy clusters, where the air is mild, and the mountains glow with colors unknown here.

"But you have not our brown cole there!" objected the Hen. "I was once in the country, with my children, in one summer that lasted five weeks. There was a sand pit, in which we could walk about and scratch; and we had the *entrée* to a garden where brown cole grew: it was so hot there that one could scarcely breathe; and then we have not all the poisonous animals that infest these warm countries of yours, and we are free from robbers. He is a villain who does not consider our country the most beautiful—he certainly does not deserve to be here!" And then the Hen wept, and went on: "I have also traveled. I rode in a coop above twelve miles; and there is no pleasure at all in traveling!"

"Yes, the Hen is a sensible woman!" said the doll Bertha. "I don't think anything of traveling among mountains, for

you only have to go up, and then down again. No, we will
go into the sand pit beyond the gate, and walk about in the
cabbage garden."

And so it was settled.

"Am I to hear some stories now?" asked little Hjalmar,
as soon as Ole Shut-Eye had sent him to sleep.

"This evening we have no time for that," replied Ole
Shut-Eye; and he spread his finest umbrella over the lad.
"Only look at these Chinese!"

And the whole umbrella looked like a great china dish, with
blue trees and pointed bridges, with little Chinese upon
them, who stood there nodding their heads.

"We must have the whole world prettily decked out for
tomorrow morning," said Ole Shut-Eye, "for that will be a
holiday—it will be Sunday. I will go to the church steeples
to see that the little church goblins are polishing the bells,
that they may sound sweetly. I will go out into the field, and
see if the breezes are blowing the dust from the grass and
leaves; and, what is the greatest work of all, I will bring
down all the stars, to polish them. I take them in my apron;
but first each one must be numbered, and the holes in which
they are placed up there must be numbered likewise, so that
they may be placed in the same grooves again; otherwise
they would not sit fast, and we should have too many
shooting stars, for one after another would fall down."

"Hark ye! Do you know, Mr. Ole Shut-Eye," said an old
Portrait which hung on the wall where Hjalmar slept, "I am
Hjalmar's great-grandfather? I thank you for telling the boy
stories; but you must not confuse his ideas. The stars cannot
come down and be polished! The stars are world-orbs, just

like our own earth, and that is just the good thing about them."

"I thank you, old great-grandfather," said Ole Shut-Eye, "I thank you! You are then the head of the family. You are the ancestral head; but I am older than you! I am an old heathen: the Romans and Greeks called me the Dream God! I have been in the noblest houses, and am admitted there still! I know how to act with great people and with small! Now you may tell your own story!" and Ole Shut-Eye took his umbrella, and went away.

"Well, well! May one not even give an opinion nowadays?" grumbled the old Portrait. And Hjalmar awoke.

SUNDAY

"Good evening!" said Ole Shut-Eye; and Hjalmar nodded, and then ran and turned his great-grandfather's Portrait against the wall, that it might not interrupt them, as it had done yesterday.

"Now you must tell me stories; about the five green peas that lived in one shell, and about the cock's foot that paid court to the hen's foot, and of the darning needle who gave herself such airs because she thought herself a working needle."

"There may be too much of a good thing!" said Ole Shut-Eye. "You know that I prefer showing you something. I will show you my own brother. His name, like mine, is Ole Shut-Eye, but he never comes to any one more than once; and he takes him to whom he comes upon his horse, and tells him stories. He only knows two. One of these is so exceedingly beautiful that no one in the world can imagine it, and the other so horrible that it cannot be described."

And then Ole Shut-Eye lifted little Hjalmar up to the window, and said—

"There you will see my brother, the other Ole Shut-Eye. They also call him Death! Do you see, he does not look so terrible as they make him in the picture books, where he is only a skeleton. No, that is silver embroidery that he has on his coat; that is a splendid hussar's uniform; a mantle of black velvet flies behind him over the horse. See how he gallops along! "

And Hjalmar saw how this Ole Shut-Eye rode away, and took young people as well as old upon his horse. Some of them he put before him, and some behind: but he always asked first, "How stands it with the mark book?" "Well," they all replied. "Yes, let me see it myself," he said. And then each one had to show him the book; and those who had "very well" and "remarkably well" written in their books, were placed in front of his horse, and a lovely story was told to them; while those who had "middling" or "tolerably well," had to sit up behind, and hear a very terrible story indeed. They trembled and wept, and wanted to jump off the horse, but this they could not do, for they had all, as it were, grown fast to it.

"But Death is a most splendid Ole Shut-Eye," said Hjalmar. "I am not afraid of him! "

"Nor need you be," replied Ole Shut-Eye; "but see that you have a good mark book! "

"Yes, that is improving! " muttered the great-grandfather's Picture. "It is of some use giving one's opinion." And now he was satisfied.

You see, that is the story of Ole Shut-Eye; and now he may tell you more himself, this evening!

The Wicked Prince

A LEGEND

Once upon a time, there was a wicked and haughty prince, whose thoughts constantly dwelt on how he might conquer all the nations of the earth, and make his name a terror to all men. He ravaged with fire and sword; his soldiers trod down the grain in the fields; they put the torch to the peasant's cottage, so that the red flame licked the very leaves from the trees, and the fruit hung roasted from the black and singed limbs. Many a poor mother, with her naked babe, hid away behind the smoking ruins, and the soldiers sought her, and found her and the child, and then began their devilish sport: the demons of the pit could do no worse; but the Prince found it all to his liking; day by day he grew mightier, his name was feared by everybody, and good fortune came upon him to his heart's content. From the conquered cities he carried away gold and great treasure, and amassed in his capital such riches as were never before found together in one place. Then he built superb palaces, temples, and arches; and whoever saw his magnificence, exclaimed, "What a great Prince!"—never thinking of the desolation he had brought over many lands, nor listening to the groans and wailings that arose from the cities which fire had laid waste.

The Prince looked upon his gold, looked upon his superb buildings, and thought, as folks did, "What a great Prince!" "But I wish to have more, much more! No power is there that can equal, much less surpass, mine!" And so he went to war with his neighbors and subdued them all. The vanquished kings he chained to his chariot with golden chains, when he drove through the streets; and when he sat down to his table, they were made to lie at his and his courtiers' feet, and eat the morsels that might be thrown to them.

Now the Prince caused his image to be set up in the market places and in the royal palaces; he would even have set it up in the temples before the altar of the Lord; but the priests said, "Prince, thou art great, but God is greater: we dare not do it."

"Well," said the wicked Prince, "then I shall conquer Him likewise!" and in his heart's pride and folly, he built an artfully contrived ship, in which he could sail through the air; it was decked with peacocks' feathers, and seemed spangled with a thousand eyes; but each eye was a gun's mouth, and the Prince sat in the midst of the ship, and, upon his touching a certain spring, a thousand bullets would dart forth, and the guns would at once be loaded afresh. Hundreds of strong eagles were harnessed to the ship, and so it flew away, up towards the sun. The earth lay far beneath; at first it appeared, with its mountains and forests, like a plowed meadow, with a tuft of green here and there peeping out from under the upturned sod; then it resembled an unrolled map; and presently it was wholly hid in mists and clouds. Higher and higher the eagles flew; when God sent forth a single one of his countless angels, at whom the wicked Prince immediately let fly a thousand bullets; but the bullets dropped like hail from the angel's shining wings, and one drop of blood—but one—dripped from one of the white pinions, and fell on the ship wherein sat the Prince; it burned itself fast there, and weighed with a weight of a thousand hundredweight, and with thundering speed tore the ship down back to the earth. The eagles' strong wings were broken, the winds roared about the Prince's head; and the clouds round about, which had sprung from the smoke of the burned cities, formed themselves into terrific shapes— anon like mile-long crab-fish, reaching out their huge claws after him—anon like rolling boulders or like fiery dragons: half dead he lay in his ship, when it finally was caught in the tangled branches of a dense forest.

"I *will* conquer God!" said he; "I have vowed it, and my will shall be done!" and during seven years he builded artfully contrived vessels, in which to sail through the air, and caused thunderbolts to be forged from the hardest of steel, wherewith to batter down heaven's battlements. From all countries, he assembled vast armies, which covered many miles of ground in length and breadth, when formed in battle array. They embarked in the artfully built vessels, and already the King himself approached his; when God sent forth a swarm of gnats—one little swarm—which buzzed about the King, and stung his face and hands. In anger he drew his sword; but he beat the void air only: the gnats he could not strike. Whereupon he commanded that costly cloths be brought, and wrapped about him, so that no gnat might reach him with its sting. It was done as he had commanded; but one little gnat had lodged itself in the folds of the inmost cloth, and crept into the King's ear and stung him; the sting smarted as fire, the poison flew up into his head; he tore himself loose, flung the cloths far away, rent his garments asunder, and danced naked before the rough and savage soldiers, who now mocked the mad Prince that had set out to besiege God, and had been himself undone by one tiny gnat.

The Swineherd

There was once a poor prince who had only a tiny kingdom, but it was big enough to allow him to marry, and he was bent upon marrying.

Now it certainly was rather bold of him to say to the Emperor's daughter, "Will you have me?" He did, however, venture to say so, for his name was known far and wide. And there were hundreds of princesses who would have said "Yes," and "Thank you, kindly," but see if *she* would!

Let us hear about it.

A rose tree grew on the grave of the Prince's father. It was such a beautiful rose tree. But it bloomed only every fifth year, and then bore only one blossom. What a rose that was! By merely smelling it one forgot all of one's cares and sorrows.

Then he had a nightingale which sang as if every lovely melody in the world dwelt in her little throat. This rose and this nightingale were to be given to the Princess, so they were put into great silver caskets and sent to her.

The Emperor had them carried before him into the great hall where the Princess was playing at "visiting" with her ladies-in-waiting—they had nothing else to do. When she saw the caskets with the gifts, she clapped her hands with delight.

"If it were only a little pussy cat!" said she. But there was the lovely rose.

"Oh, how exquisitely it is made!" said all the ladies-in-waiting.

"It is more than beautiful," said the Emperor. "It is neatly made." But the Princess touched it, and then she was ready to cry.

"Fie, papa!" she said. "It is not made. It is a real one."

"Fie," said all the ladies-in-waiting. "It is a real one."

"Well, let us see what there is in the other casket, before we get angry," said the Emperor, and out came the nightingale. It sang so beautifully that at first no one could find anything to say against it.

"*Superbe! charmant!*" said the ladies-in-waiting, for they all had a smattering of French; one spoke it worse than the other.

"How that bird reminds me of our lamented Empress' musical box," said an old courtier. "Ah yes, they are the same tunes and the same beautiful execution."

"So they are," said the Emperor, crying like a little child.

"I should hardly think it could be a real one," said the Princess.

"Yes, it is a real one," said those who had brought it.

"Oh, let that bird fly away then," said the Princess, and she would not hear of allowing the Prince to come. But he was not to be crushed. He stained his face brown and black and, pressing his cap over his eyes, he knocked at the door.

"Good morning, Emperor," said he. "Can I be taken into service in the palace?"

"Well, there are so many wishing to do that," said the Emperor. "But let me see. Yes, I need somebody to look after the pigs. We have so many of them."

So the Prince was made imperial swineherd. A horrid little room was given him near the pigsties, and here he had to live. He sat busily at work all day, and by the evening he

had made a beautiful little cooking pot. It had bells all
round it, and when the pot boiled, they tinkled delightfully
and played the old tune:

> *"Ach du lieber Augustin,*
> *Alles ist weg, weg, weg!"* •

But the greatest of all its charms was that by holding
one's finger in the steam, one could immediately smell all
the dinners that were being cooked at every stove in the
town. Now this was a very different matter from a rose.

The Princess came walking along with all her ladies-in-
waiting, and when she heard the tune she stopped and
looked pleased, for she could play "Ach du lieber Augustin"
herself. It was her only tune, and she could only play it
with one finger.

"Why, that is my tune," she said. "This must be a
cultivated swineherd. Ask him what the instrument costs."

So one of the ladies-in-waiting had to go into his room,
but before she entered she put on wooden clog-shoes.

"How much do you want for the pot?" she asked.

"I must have ten kisses from the Princess," said the
swineherd.

"Heaven preserve us!" said the lady.

"I won't take less," said the swineherd.

"Well, what does he say?" asked the Princess.

"I really cannot tell you," said the lady-in-waiting. "It
is so shocking."

"Then you must whisper it." And she whispered it.

"He is a wretch!" said the Princess and went away at
once. But she had only gone a little way when she heard
the bells tinkling beautifully:

> *"Ach du lieber Augustin."*

• Alas, dear Augustin,
  All is lost, lost, lost!

"Go and ask him if he will take ten kisses from the ladies-in-waiting."

"No, thank you," said the swineherd. "Ten kisses from the Princess, or I keep my pot."

"How tiresome it is," said the Princess. "Then you will have to stand round me, so that no one may see."

So the ladies-in-waiting stood round her and spread out their skirts while the swineherd took his ten kisses, and then the pot was hers.

What a delight it was to them! The pot was kept on the boil day and night. They knew what was cooking on every stove in the town, from the chamberlain's to the shoemaker's. The ladies-in-waiting danced about and clapped their hands.

"We know who has sweet soup and pancakes for dinner, and who has cutlets. How amusing it is."

"Highly interesting," said the mistress of the robes.

"Yes, but hold your tongues, for I am the Emperor's daughter."

"Heaven preserve us!" they all said.

The swineherd—that is to say, the Prince, only nobody knew that he was not a real swineherd—did not let the day pass in idleness, and he now constructed a rattle. When it was swung round it played all the waltzes, galops and jig tunes ever heard since the creation of the world.

"But this is *superbe!*" said the Princess, as she walked by. "I have never heard finer compositions. Go and ask him what the instrument costs, but let us have no more kissing."

"He wants a hundred kisses from the Princess," said the lady-in-waiting.

"I think he is mad!" said the Princess, and she went away, but she had not gone far when she stopped.

"One must encourage art," she said. "I am the Emperor's daughter. Tell him he can have ten kisses, the same as yesterday, and he can take the others from the ladies-in-waiting."

"Out you go!" cried the Emperor to both the prince and the princess!

"But we don't like that at all," said the ladies.

"Oh, nonsense! If I can kiss him you can do the same. Remember that I pay you wages as well as give you board and lodging." So the lady-in-waiting had to go again.

"A hundred kisses from the Princess, or let each keep his own."

"Stand in front of me," said she, and all the ladies stood round while he kissed her.

"Whatever is the meaning of that crowd round the pigsties?" said the Emperor as he stepped out on to the veranda. He rubbed his eyes and put on his spectacles. "Why, it is the ladies-in-waiting. What game are they up to? I must go and see!" So he pulled up the heels of his slippers for they were shoes which he had trodden down.

Bless us, what a hurry he was in! When he got into the yard he walked very softly, and the ladies were so busy counting the kisses, so that there should be fair play, and neither too few nor too many kisses, that they never heard the Emperor. He stood on tiptoe.

"What is all this?" he said when he saw what was going on, and he hit them on the head with his slipper just as the swineherd was taking his eighty-sixth kiss.

"Out you go!" said the Emperor. He was very furious, and he put both the Princess and the Prince out of his realm.

There she stood crying, and the swineherd scolded, and the rain poured down in torrents.

"Oh, miserable creature that I am!" said the Princess. "If only I had accepted the handsome Prince. Oh, how unhappy I am!"

The swineherd went behind a tree, wiped the black and brown stain from his face, and threw away his ugly clothes. When he stepped out dressed as a prince, he was so handsome that the Princess could not help curtseying to him.

"I am come to despise thee," he said. "Thou wouldst not have an honorable prince. Thou couldst not prize the rose or the nightingale. But thou wouldst kiss the swineherd for a trumpery musical box! As thou hast made thy bed, so must thou lie upon it."

Then he went back into his own little kingdom and shut and locked the door. So she had to stand outside and sing in earnest:

> *" Ach du lieber Augustin,*
> *Alles ist weg, weg, weg!"*

Hans Clodhopper

There was once an old mansion in the country in which lived an old squire with his two sons, and these two sons were too clever by half. They had made up their minds to propose to the King's daughter. And they ventured to do so because she had made it known that she would take any man for a husband who had most to say for himself.

These two took a week over their preparations. It was all the time they had for it, but it was quite enough with all their accomplishments, which were most useful. One of them knew the Latin dictionary by heart, as well as the town newspapers for three years, either forwards or backwards. The second one had made himself acquainted with all the statutes of the Corporations and what every alderman had to know, so he thought he was competent to talk about affairs of state. And he also knew how to embroider harnesses, for he was clever with his fingers.

"I shall win the King's daughter," they both said, and their father gave each of them a beautiful horse. The one who could repeat the dictionary and the newspapers had a coal-black horse, while the one who was learned in guilds and embroideries had a milk-white one. Then they smeared the corners of their mouths with oil to make them more flexible. All the servants were assembled in the courtyards to see them mount, but just then the third brother came up—for there were three. Only nobody made any account of this one, Hans Clodhopper, as he had no accomplishments like his brothers.

"Where are you going in your fine clothes?" he asked.

"To court, to talk ourselves into favor with the Princess. Haven't you heard the news which is being drummed all over the country?" And then they told him the news.

"Preserve us! Then I must go too," said Hans Clodhopper. But his brothers laughed and rode away.

"Father, give me a horse. I want to get married too. If she takes me she takes me, and if she doesn't take me, I shall take her all the same."

"Stuff and nonsense!" said his father. "I will give no horse to you. Why, you have got nothing to say for yourself, but your brothers are fine fellows."

"If I mayn't have a horse," said Hans Clodhopper, "I'll take the billy goat. He is my own and he can carry me very well!" And he seated himself astride the billy goat, dug his heels into its sides, and galloped off down the highroad. Whew! what a pace they went at.

"Here I come," shouted Hans Clodhopper, and he sang till the air rang.

The brothers rode on in silence. They did not say a word to each other, for they had to store up every good idea which they wanted to produce later on, and their speeches had to be very carefully thought out.

"Hallo!" shouted Hans Clodhopper. "Here I come. See what I've found on the road!" And he showed them a dead crow.

"What on earth will you do with that, Clodhopper?" said they.

"I will give it to the King's daughter."

"Yes, I would do that," said they, and they rode on laughing.

"Hallo, here I come! See what I have found! One doesn't

find such a thing as this every day on the road." The brothers turned round to see what it was.

"Clodhopper," said they, "it's nothing but an old wooden shoe with the upper part broken off. Is the Princess to have that too?"

"Yes indeed she is," said Hans, and the brothers again rode on laughing.

"Hallo, hallo, here I am!" shouted Hans Clodhopper. "Now this is something wonderful!"

"What have you found this time?" asked the brothers.

"Won't the Princess be delighted!"

"Why," said the brothers, "it's only sand picked up out of the ditch!"

"Yes, that it is," said Hans Clodhopper, "and the finest kind of sand, too. You can hardly hold it." And he filled his pockets with it. His brothers rode on as fast as they could, and arrived at the town gates a whole hour before him. At the gate suitors received tickets in the order of their arrival, and they were arranged in rows, six in each file and so close together that they could not move their arms. This was a very good thing, or they would have torn each other's garments off, merely because one stood in front of the other. All the other inhabitants of the town stood round the castle, peeping in at the windows to see the King's daughter receive the suitors. And as each one of them came into the room he lost the power of speech.

"No good," said the Princess. "Away with him!"

Now came the brother who could repeat the dictionary, but he had entirely forgotten it while standing in the ranks. The floor creaked and the ceiling was made of looking glass, so that he saw himself standing on his head. And at every window sat three clerks and an alderman, who wrote down all that was said, so that it might be sent to the papers at once and sold for a halfpenny at the street corners. It was

terrible, and the stoves had been heated to such a degree that
they got red-hot at the top.

"It is terribly hot in here," said the suitor.

"That is because my father is roasting cockerels today,"
said the Princess.

Bah! There he stood like a fool. He had not expected a
conversation of this kind, and he could not think of a word
to say, just when he wanted to be specially witty.

"No good," said the King's daughter. "Away with him!"
And he had to go.

Then came the second brother. "There's a fearful heat
here," said he.

"Yes, we are roasting cockerels today," said the King's
daughter.

"What did—what?" said he. And all the reporters duly
wrote, "What did—what."

"No good," said the King's daughter. "Away with him!"

Then came Hans Clodhopper. He rode the billy goat right
into the room.

"What a burning heat you have here," said he.

"That is because I am roasting cockerels," said the King's
daughter.

"That is very convenient," said Hans Clodhopper. "Then
I suppose I can get a crow roasted too."

"Yes, very well," said the King's daughter. "But have you
anything to roast it in? I have neither pot nor pan."

"But I have," said Hans Clodhopper. "Here is a cooking
pot." And he brought out the wooden shoe and put the
crow into it.

"Why you have enough for a whole meal," said the King's
daughter. "But where shall we get any dripping to baste
it with?"

"Oh, I have some in my pocket," said Hans Clodhopper.
"I have enough and to spare." And he poured a little of the
sand out of his pocket.

"Now I like that," said the Princess. "You have an answer for everything, and you have something to say for yourself. I will have you for a husband. But do you know that every word we have said will be in the paper tomorrow? For at every window sit three clerks and an alderman, and the alderman is the worst, for he doesn't understand." She said this to frighten him. All the clerks sniggered and made blots of ink on the floor.

"Oh, those are the gentry!" said Hans Clodhopper. "Then I must give the alderman the best thing I have." And he turned out his pockets and threw the sand in his face.

"That was cleverly done," said the Princess. "I couldn't have done it, but I will try to learn."

So Hans Clodhopper became King, gained a wife and a crown, and sat upon the throne. We have this straight out of the alderman's newspaper, but it is not to be depended upon.

The Love Affair of the Top and the Ball

A Top and a little Ball were together in a drawer among some other toys; and the Top said to the Ball—

"Shall we not be lovers, as we live together in the same box?"

But the Ball, which had a coat of morocco leather, and was just as conceited as any fine lady, would make no answer to such a proposal. The next day came the little boy to whom the toys belonged: he painted the Top red and yellow, and hammered a brass nail into it; and it looked splendid when the Top turned round.

"Look at me!" he cried to the little Ball. "What do you say now? Shall we not be engaged to each other? We suit one another so well! You jump and I dance! No one could be happier than we two should be."

"Indeed! Do you think so?" replied the little Ball. "Perhaps you do not know that my papa and my mamma were morocco slippers, and that I have a Spanish cork inside me?"

"Yes, but I am made of mahogany," said the Top; "and the mayor himself turned me. He has a turning lathe of his own, and it amuses him greatly."

"Can I depend on that?" asked the little Ball.

"May I never be whipped again if it is not true!" replied the Top.

"You can speak well for yourself," observed the Ball,

"but I cannot grant your request. I am as good as engaged to a swallow: every time I leap up into the air he puts his head out of the nest and says, 'Will you?' And now I have silently said 'Yes,' and that is as good as half engaged; but I promise I will never forget you."

"Yes, that will be much good!" said the Top.

And they spoke no more to each other.

Next day the Ball was taken out by the boy. The Top saw how she flew high into air, like a bird; at last one could no longer see her. Each time she came back again, but gave a high leap when she touched the earth, and that was done either from her longing to mount up again, or because she had a Spanish cork in her body. But the ninth time the little Ball remained absent, and did not come back again; and the boy sought and sought, but she was gone.

"I know very well where she is!" sighed the Top. "She is in the Swallow's nest, and has married the Swallow!"

The more the Top thought of this, the more it longed for the Ball. Just because it could not get the Ball, its love increased; and the fact that the Ball had chosen another formed a peculiar feature in the case. So the Top danced round and hummed, but always thought of the little Ball, which became more and more beautiful in his fancy. Thus several years went by, and now it was an old love.

And the Top was no longer young! But one day he was gilt all over; never had he looked so handsome; he was now a golden Top, and sprang till he hummed again. Yes, that was something worth seeing! But all at once he sprang too high, and—he was gone!

They looked and looked, even in the cellar, but he was not to be found. Where could he be?

He had jumped into the dust box, where all kinds of things were lying: cabbage stalks, sweepings, and dust that had fallen down from the roof.

" Here's a nice place to lie in! The gilding will soon leave me here. Among what a rabble have I alighted! "

And then he looked sideways at a long leafless cabbage stump, and at a curious round thing like an old apple; but it was not an apple—it was an old Ball, which had lain for years in the roof gutter and was quite saturated with water.

" Thank goodness, here comes one of us, with whom one can talk! " said the little Ball, and looked at the gilt Top. " I am really morocco, worked by maidens' hands, and have a Spanish cork within me; but no one would think it, to look at me. I was very near marrying a swallow, but I fell into the gutter on the roof, and have lain there full five years, and become quite wet through. You may believe me, that's a long time for a young girl."

But the Top said nothing. He thought of his old love; and the more he heard, the clearer it became to him that this was she. Then came the servant girl, and wanted to turn out the dust box. " Aha! there's a gilt top! " she cried. And so the Top was brought again to notice and honor, but nothing was heard of the little Ball. And the Top spoke no more of his old love; for that dies away when the beloved object has lain for five years in a roof gutter and got wet through; yes, one does not know her again when one meets her in the dust box.

The Nightingale

In China, as you know, the Emperor is a Chinese and all the people around him are Chinese too. It is many years since the story I am going to tell you happened, but that is all the more reason for telling it, lest it should be forgotten.

The Emperor's palace was the most beautiful thing in the world. It was made entirely of finest porcelain, which was very costly, and so fragile that it could be touched only with the very greatest of care. The most extraordinary flowers were to be seen in the garden. The most beautiful ones had little silver bells tied to them which tinkled perpetually, so that no one could pass the flowers without looking at them. Every little detail in the garden had been most carefully thought out, and it was so big that even the gardener himself did not know where it ended.

If one went on walking, one came to beautiful woods with lofty trees and deep lakes. The woods extended to the sea, which was deep and blue, deep enough for large ships to sail up right under the branches of the trees. Among these trees lived a nightingale, which sang so deliciously that even the poor fisherman, who had plenty of other things to do, lay still to listen to it when he was out at night drawing in his nets.

"Heavens, how beautiful it is," he said, but then he had to attend to his business and forgot it. The next night when he heard it again he would again exclaim, "Heavens, how beautiful it is."

Travelers came to the Emperor's capital from every country in the world. They admired everything very much, especially the palace and the gardens, but when they heard the nightingale they all said, "This is better than anything."

When they got home they described it, and learned men wrote many books about the town, the palace, and the garden. But nobody forgot the nightingale—it was always put above everything else. Those among them who were poets wrote the most beautiful poems, all about the nightingale in the woods by the deep blue sea. These books went all over the world, and in course of time some of them reached the Emperor. He sat in his golden chair reading and reading, and nodding his head, well pleased to hear such beautiful descriptions of the town, the palace, and the garden. "But the nightingale is the best of all," he read.

"What is this?" said the Emperor. "The nightingale? Why, I know nothing about it. Is there such a bird in my kingdom, and in my own garden, and I have never heard of it? Imagine my having to discover this from a book."

Then he called his gentleman-in-waiting, who was so grand that when anyone of a lower rank dared to speak to him or to ask him a question, he would only answer, "P," which means nothing at all.

"There is said to be a very wonderful bird called a nightingale here," said the Emperor. "They say that it is better than anything else in all my great kingdom. Why have I never been told anything about it?"

"I have never heard it mentioned," said the gentleman-in-waiting. "It has never been presented at court."

"I wish it to appear here this evening to sing to me," said the Emperor. "The whole world knows what I am possessed of, and I know nothing about it!"

"I have never heard it mentioned before," said the

gentleman-in-waiting. "I will seek it, and I will find it." But where was it to be found? The gentleman-in-waiting ran upstairs and downstairs and in and out of all the rooms and corridors. No one of all those he met had ever heard anything about the nightingale. So the gentleman-in-waiting ran back to the Emperor and said that it must be a myth, invented by the writers of the books. "Your Imperial Majesty must not believe everything that is written! Books are often mere inventions, even if they do not belong to what we call the black art."

"But the book in which I read it was sent to me by the powerful Emperor of Japan. Therefore it can't be untrue. I will hear this nightingale. I insist upon its being here tonight. I extend my most gracious protection to it, and if it is not forthcoming, I will have the whole court trampled upon after supper."

"Tsing-pe!" said the gentleman-in-waiting, and away he ran again, up and down all the stairs, in and out of all the rooms and corridors. Half the court ran with him, for none of them wished to be trampled on. There was much questioning about this nightingale, which was known to all the outside world but to no one at court.

At last they found a poor little maid in the kitchen, who said, "Oh heavens! The nightingale? I know it very well. Yes indeed, it can sing. Every evening I am allowed to take broken meat to my poor sick mother who lives down by the shore. On my way back, when I am tired I rest awhile in the wood, and then I hear the nightingale. Its song brings the tears into my eyes. I feel as if my mother were kissing me."

"Little kitchen maid," said the gentleman-in-waiting, "I will procure you a permanent position in the kitchen and permission to see the Emperor dining, if you will take us to the nightingale. It is commanded to appear at court tonight."

Then they all went out into the woods where the night-

ingale usually sang. Half the court was there. As they were
going along at their best pace, a cow began to bellow.

" Oh," said a young courtier, "there we have it. What
wonderful power for such a little creature. I have certainly
heard it before."

" No, those are the cows bellowing. We are a long way
from the place." Then frogs began to croak in the marsh.

" How beautiful! " said the Chinese chaplain. "It is just
like the tinkling of church bells."

" No, those are the frogs," said the little kitchen maid.
" But I think we shall soon hear it now."

Then the nightingale began to sing.

" Listen, listen! There it sits," said the little girl. And she
pointed to a little gray bird up among the branches.

" Is it possible? " said the gentleman-in-waiting. "I should
never have thought it was like that. How common it looks.
Seeing so many grand people must have frightened all its
colors away."

" Little nightingale," called the kitchen maid quite loud,
" Our Gracious Emperor wishes you to sing to him."

" With the greatest pleasure," said the nightingale, warbling
away in the most delightful fashion.

" It is just like crystal bells," said the gentleman-in-waiting.
" Look at its little throat, how active it is. It is extraordinary
that we have never heard it before. I am sure it will be a
great success at court."

" Shall I sing again to the Emperor? " said the nightingale,
who thought he was present.

" My precious little nightingale," said the gentleman-in-
waiting, " I have the honor to command your attendance at
a court festival tonight, where you will charm His Gracious
Majesty the Emperor with your fascinating singing."

" It sounds best among the trees," said the nightingale,
but it went with them willingly when it heard that the
Emperor wished it.

The palace had been brightened up for the occasion. The walls and the floors, which were all of china, shone by the light of many thousand golden lamps. The most beautiful flowers, all of the tinkling kind, were arranged in the corridors. There was hurrying to and fro, and a great draught, but this was just what made the bells ring. One's ears were full of the tinkling. In the middle of the large reception room where the Emperor sat, a golden rod had been fixed, on which the nightingale was to perch. The whole court was assembled, and the little kitchen maid had been permitted to stand behind the door, as she now had the actual title of Cook. They were all dressed in their best. Everybody's eyes were turned towards the little gray bird at which the Emperor was nodding.

The nightingale sang delightfully, and the tears came into the Emperor's eyes and rolled down his cheeks. And when the nightingale sang more beautifully than ever, its notes melted all hearts. The Emperor was so charmed that he said the nightingale should have his gold slipper to wear round its neck. But the nightingale declined with thanks—it had already been sufficiently rewarded.

"I have seen tears in the eyes of the Emperor," he said. "That is my richest reward. The tears of the Emperor have a wonderful power. God knows I am sufficiently recompensed." And it again burst into its sweet heavenly song.

"That is the most delightful coquetting I have ever seen! " said the ladies. And they took some water into their mouths to try and make the same gurgling, when anyone spoke to them, thinking so to equal the nightingale. Even the lackeys and the chambermaids announced that they were satisfied, and that is saying a great deal. They are always the most difficult people to please. Yes indeed, the nightingale had made a sensation. It was to stay at court now, and have its own cage, as well as liberty to walk out twice a day and once in the night. It always had twelve footmen, with each

The gift was a man-made nightingale, covered with diamonds, rubies, and sapphires!

one holding a ribbon which was tied round its leg. There was not much pleasure in an outing of that sort.

The whole town talked about the marvelous bird. If two people met, one said to the other "Night," and the other answered "Gale." And then they sighed, perfectly understanding each other. Eleven cheesemongers' children were named after it, but not one among them could sing anything.

One day a large parcel came for the Emperor. Outside was written the word "Nightingale."

"Here we have another new book about this celebrated bird," said the Emperor. But it was not a book. It was a little work of art in a box, an artificial nightingale exactly like the living one, except that it was studded all over with diamonds, rubies, and sapphires.

When the artificial bird was wound up, it could sing one of the songs the real one sang, and it wagged its tail, which glittered with silver and gold. A ribbon was tied round its neck on which was written, "The Emperor of Japan's nightingale is very poor compared to the Emperor of China's."

Everybody said, "Oh, how beautiful!" And the person who brought the artificial bird immediately received the title of Imperial Nightingale-Carrier-in-Chief.

"Now, they must sing together. What a duet that will be!"

Then they had to sing together, but they did not get on very well, for the real nightingale sang in its own way and the artificial one could only sing waltzes.

"There is no fault in that," said the music master, "It is perfectly in time and correct in every way."

Then the artificial bird had to sing alone. It was just as great a success as the real one, and it was much prettier to look at, because it glittered like bracelets and breastpins.

It sang the same tune three and thirty times over, and yet it was not tired. People would willingly have heard it from the beginning again, but the Emperor said that the real one must have a turn now. But where was it? No one had noticed that it had flown out of the open window, back to its own green woods.

" What is the meaning of this? " said the Emperor.

All the courtiers railed at it and said it was a most ungrateful bird.

" We have got the best bird though," said they, and then the artificial bird had to sing again. This was the thirty-fourth time that they had heard the same tune, but they did not know it thoroughly even yet because it was so difficult.

The music master praised the bird tremendously and insisted that it was better than the real nightingale, not only on the outside with all its diamonds, but inside too.

" You see, my ladies and gentlemen, and the Emperor before all, in the real nightingale you never know what you will hear, but in the artificial one everything is decided beforehand. So it is, and so it must remain. It can't be otherwise. You can account for things: you can open it and show the human ingenuity in arranging how the waltzes go, and how one note follows upon another."

" Those are exactly my opinions," they all said, and the music master got leave to show the bird to the public next Sunday. They were also to hear it sing, said the Emperor. So they heard it, and all became as enthusiastic over it as if they had drunk themselves merry on tea, because that is a thoroughly Chinese habit.

Then they all said, " Oh! " and stuck their forefingers in the air and nodded their heads. But the poor fisherman who had heard the real nightingale said, " It sounds very nice, and it is very nearly like the real one, but there is something wanting. I don't know what." The real nightingale was banished from the kingdom.

The artificial bird had its place on a silken cushion, close to the Emperor's bed. All the presents it had received of gold and precious jewels were scattered round it. Its title had risen to be Chief Imperial Singer-of-the-Bed-Chamber. In rank it stood number one on the left side, for the Emperor reckoned that side where the heart was seated was the important one. And even an Emperor's heart is on the left side.

The music master wrote five and twenty volumes about the artificial bird. The treatise was very long, and was written in all the most difficult Chinese characters. Everybody said they had read and understood it, for otherwise they would have been reckoned stupid, and then their bodies would have been trampled upon.

Things went on in this way for a whole year. The Emperor, the court, and all the other Chinese knew every little gurgle in the song of the artificial bird by heart. But they liked it all the better for this, and they could all join in the song themselves. Even the street boys sang "Zizizi! cluck, cluck, cluck!" And the Emperor sang it too.

But one evening, when the bird was singing its best and the Emperor was lying in bed listening to it, something gave way inside the bird with a "whizz." "Whirr!" went all the wheels, and the music stopped.

The Emperor jumped out of bed and sent for his private physicians, but what good could they do? Then they sent for the watchmaker, who after a good deal of talk and examination got the works to go again somehow. But he said the bird would have to be spared as much as possible, because it was so worn out, and that he could not renew the works so as to be sure of the tune. This was a great blow! They now dared to let the artificial bird sing only once a year, and hardly that. But then the music master made a little speech using all the most difficult Chinese words. He said it was just as good as ever, and his saying it made it so.

Five years passed, and then a great grief came upon the nation. They were all very fond of their Emperor, and now he was ill and could not live, it was said. A new Emperor was already chosen, and people stood about in the street and asked the gentleman-in-waiting how the Emperor was getting on.

"P," answered he, shaking his head.

The Emperor lay pale and cold in his gorgeous bed. The courtiers thought he was dead, and they all went off to pay their respects to their new Emperor. The lackeys ran off to talk matters over, and the chambermaids gave a great coffee party. Cloth had been laid down in all the rooms and corridors so as to deaden the sounds of footsteps, so it was very, very quiet. But the Emperor was not dead yet. He lay stiff and pale in the gorgeous bed with velvet hangings and heavy golden tassels. There was an open window high above him, and the moon streamed in upon the Emperor and the artificial bird beside him.

The poor Emperor could hardly breathe. He seemed to have a weight on his chest. He opened his eyes and then he saw that it was Death sitting upon his chest, wearing his golden crown. In one hand he held the Emperor's golden sword, and in the other his Imperial banner. From among the folds of the velvet hangings peered many curious faces. Some were hideous, others gentle and pleasant. They were all the Emperor's good and bad deeds, which now looked him in the face when Death was weighing him down.

"Do you remember that?" whispered one after the other. "Do you remember this?" And they told him so many things that the perspiration poured down his face.

"I never knew that," said the Emperor. "Music, music! Sound the great Chinese drums," he cried, "that I may not hear what they are saying." But they went on and on, and Death sat nodding his head like a Chinese at everything that was said. "Music, music!" shrieked the Emperor. "You precious little golden bird, sing, sing! I have loaded you with precious stones, and even hung my own golden slipper round your neck. Sing, I tell you, sing! "

But the bird stood silent. There was nobody to wind it

up, so of course it could not go. Death continued to fix the great empty sockets of its eyes upon him, and all was silent, terribly silent.

Suddenly, close to the window there was a burst of lovely song. It was the living nightingale, perched on a branch outside. It had heard of the Emperor's need and had come to bring comfort and hope to him. As it sang, the faces round became fainter, and the blood coursed with fresh vigor in the Emperor's veins and through his feeble limbs. Even Death himself listened to the song and said, " Go on, little nightingale, go on! "

" Yes, if you give me the gorgeous golden sword. Yes, if you give me the Imperial banner. Yes, if you give me the Emperor's crown."

And Death gave back each of these treasures for a song, and the nightingale went on singing. It sang about the quiet churchyard where the roses bloom, where the elder flowers scent the air, and where the fresh grass is ever moistened anew by the tears of the mourners. This song brought to Death a longing for his own garden, and like a cold gray mist he passed out of the window.

" Thanks, thanks! " said the Emperor. " You heavenly little bird, I know you. I banished you from my kingdom, and yet you have charmed the evil visions away from my bed by your song, and even Death away from my heart. How can I ever repay you? "

" You have rewarded me," said the nightingale. " I brought tears to your eyes the very first time I ever sang to you, and I shall never forget it. Those are the jewels which gladden the heart of a singer. But sleep now, and wake up fresh and strong. I will sing to you."

Then it sang again, and the Emperor fell into a sweet refreshing sleep. The sun shone in at his window, and he awoke refreshed and well. None of his attendants had yet come back to him, for they thought he was dead, but the nightingale still sat there singing.

"You must always stay with me," said the Emperor. "You shall sing only when you like, and I will break the artificial bird into a thousand pieces."

"Don't do that," said the nightingale. "It did all the good it could. Keep it as you have always done. I can't build my nest and live in this palace, but let me come whenever I like. Then I will sit on the branch in the evening and sing to you. I will sing to cheer you and to make you thoughtful too. I will sing to you of the happy ones and of those that suffer. I will sing about the good and the evil, which are kept hidden from you. The little singing bird flies far and wide, to the poor fisherman and to the peasant's home, to numbers who are far from you and your court. I love your heart more than your crown, and yet there is an odor of sanctity round the crown too! I will come, and I will sing to you. But you must promise me one thing."

"Everything!" said the Emperor, who stood there in his imperial robes which he had just put on, and he held the sword heavy with gold upon his heart.

"Only one thing I ask you. Tell no one that you have a little bird who tells you everything. It will be better so."

Then the nightingale flew away. The attendants came in to look after their dead Emperor—and there he stood, bidding them "Good morning!"

The Ugly Duckling

It was so glorious out in the country; it was summer; the cornfields were yellow, the oats were green, the hay had been put up in stacks in the green meadows, and the stork went about on his long red legs and chattered Egyptian, for this was the language he had learned from his good mother. All around the fields and meadows were great forests, and in the midst of these forests lay deep lakes. Yes, it was right glorious out in the country. In the midst of the sunshine there lay an old farm, with deep canals about it, and from the wall down to the water grew great burdocks, so high that little children could stand upright under the loftiest of them. It was just as wild there as in the deepest wood, and here sat a Duck upon her nest; she had to hatch her ducklings; but she was almost tired out before the little ones came; and then she so seldom had visitors. The other ducks liked better to swim about in the canals than to run up to sit down under a burdock, and cackle with her.

At last one eggshell after another burst open. "Piep! piep!" it cried, and in all the eggs there were little creatures that stuck out their heads.

"Quack! quack!" they said; and they all came quacking out as fast as they could, looking all round them under the green leaves; and the mother let them look as much as they chose, for green is good for the eye.

" How wide the world is! " said all the young ones, for they certainly had much more room now than when they were in the eggs.

" D'ye think this is all the world? " said the mother. " That stretches far across the other side of the garden, quite into the parson's field; but I have never been there yet. I hope you are all together," and she stood up. " No, I have not all. The largest egg still lies there. How long is that to last? I am really tired of it." And she sat down again.

" Well, how goes it? " asked an old Duck who had come to pay her a visit.

" It lasts a long time with that one egg," said the Duck who sat there. " It will not burst. Now, only look at the others; are they not the prettiest little ducks one could possibly see? They are all like their father: the rogue, he never comes to see me."

" Let me see the egg which will not burst," said the old visitor. " You may be sure it is a turkey's egg. I was once cheated in that way, and had much anxiety and trouble with the young ones, for they are afraid of the water. Must I say it to you, I could not get them to venture in. I quacked and I clacked, but it was no use. Let me see the egg. Yes, that's a turkey's egg. Let it lie there, and teach the other children to swim."

" I think I will sit on it a little longer," said the Duck. " I've sat so long now that I can sit a few days more."

" Just as you please," said the old Duck; and she went away.

At last the great egg burst. " Piep! piep! " said the little one, and crept forth. It was very large and very ugly. The Duck looked at it.

" It's a very large duckling," said she; " none of the others look like that: can it really be a turkey chick? Well, we shall soon find out. It must go into the water, even if I have to thrust it in myself."

The next day, it was bright, beautiful weather; the sun shone on all the green trees. The Mother Duck went down to the canal with all her family. Splash! she jumped into the water. "Quack! quack!" she said, and one duckling after another plunged in. The water closed over their heads, but they came up in an instant, and swam capitally; their legs went of themselves, and were all in the water. The ugly gray Duckling swam with them.

"No, it's not a turkey," said she; "look how well it can use its legs, and how straight it holds itself. It is my own child! On the whole it's quite pretty, if one looks at it rightly. Quack! quack! come with me, and I'll lead you out into the great world, and present you in the duck yard; but keep close to me, so that no one may tread on you, and take care of the cats!"

And so they came into the duck yard. There was a terrible riot going on in there, for two families were quarreling about an eel's head, and the cat got it after all.

"See, that's how it goes in the world!" said the Mother Duck; and she whetted her beak, for she too wanted the eel's head. "Only use your legs," she said. "See that you can bustle about, and bow your heads before the old Duck yonder. She's the grandest of all here; she's of Spanish blood—that's why she's so fat; and d'ye see? she has a red rag round her leg; that's something particularly fine, and the greatest distinction a duck can enjoy: it signifies that one does not want to lose her, and that she's to be known by the animals and by men too. Shake yourselves—don't turn in your toes; a well-brought-up duck turns its toes quite out, just like father and mother—so! Now bend your necks and say 'Quack!'"

And they did so: but the other ducks round about looked at them, and said quite boldly—

"Look there! now we're to have these hanging on, as if there were not enough of us already! And—fie!—how that

Duckling yonder looks; we won't stand that!" And one Duck
flew up at it, and bit it in the neck.

"Let it alone," said the mother; "it does no harm to anyone."

"Yes, but it's too large and peculiar," said the Duck who
had bitten it; "and therefore it must be put down."

"Those are pretty children that the mother has there," said
the old Duck with the rag round her leg. "They're all pretty
but that one; that was rather unlucky. I wish she could bear
it over again."

"That cannot be done, my lady," replied the Mother Duck.
"It is not pretty, but it has a really good disposition, and
swims as well as any other; yes, I may even say it swims
better. I think it will grow up pretty, and become smaller
in time; it has lain too long in the egg, and therefore is not
properly shaped." And then she pinched it in the neck, and
smoothed its feathers. "Moreover it is a drake," she said,
"and therefore it is not so much consequence. I think he will
be very strong: he makes his way already."

"The other ducklings are graceful enough," said the old
Duck. "Make yourself at home; and if you find an eel's
head, you may bring it to me."

And now they were at home. But the poor Duckling which
had crept last out of the egg, and looked so ugly, was bitten
and pushed and jeered, as much by the ducks as by the
chickens.

"It is too big!" they all said. And the turkey cock, who
had been born with spurs, and therefore thought himself an
emperor, blew himself up like a ship in full sail, and bore
straight down upon it; then he gobbled and grew quite red
in the face. The poor Duckling did not know where it
should stand or walk; it was quite melancholy because it
looked ugly, and was the butt of the whole duck yard.

So it went on the first day; and afterwards it became worse
and worse. The poor Duckling was hunted about by every
one; even its brothers and sisters were quite angry with it,

and said, "If the cat would only catch you, you ugly
creature!" And the mother said, "If you were only far
away!" And the ducks bit it, and the chickens beat it, and
the girl who had to feed the poultry kicked at it with her
foot.

Then it ran and flew over the fence, and the little birds in
the bushes flew up in fear.

"That is because I am so ugly!" thought the Duckling;
and it shut its eyes, but flew on further; and so it came out
into the great moor, where the wild ducks lived. Here it
lay the whole night long; and it was weary and downcast.

Towards morning the wild ducks flew up, and looked at
their new companion.

"What sort of a one are you?" they asked; and the
Duckling turned in every direction, and bowed as well as it
could. "You are remarkably ugly!" said the wild ducks.
"But that is nothing to us, so long as you do not marry into
our family."

Poor thing! it certainly did not think of marrying, and only
hoped to obtain leave to lie among the reeds and drink
some of the swamp water.

Thus it lay two whole days; then came thither two wild
geese, or, properly speaking, two wild ganders. It was not
long since each had crept out of an egg, and that's why they
were so saucy.

"Listen, comrade," said one of them. "You're so ugly that
I like you. Will you go with us, and become a bird of
passage? Near here, in another moor, there are a few sweet
lovely wild geese, all unmarried, and all able to say 'Rap!'
you've a chance of making your fortune, ugly as you are."

"Piff! paff!" resounded through the air; and the two
ganders fell down dead in the swamp, and the water became
blood red. "Piff! paff!" it sounded again, and the whole flock
of wild geese rose up from the reeds. And then there was
another report. A great hunt was going on. The sportsmen

were lying in wait all round the moor, and some were even
sitting up in the branches of the trees, which spread far over
the reeds. The blue smoke rose up like clouds among the
dark trees, and was wafted far away across the water; and
the hunting dogs came—splash, splash!—into the swamp,
and the rushes and the reeds bent down on every side. That
was a fright for the poor Duckling! It turned its head, and
put it under its wing; but at that moment a frightful great
dog stood close by the Duckling. His tongue hung far out
of his mouth, and his eyes gleamed horrible and ugly; he
thrust out his nose close against the Duckling, showed his
sharp teeth, and—splash, splash!—on he went, without
seizing it.

" O, Heaven be thanked! " sighed the Duckling. " I am so
ugly, that even the dog does not like to bite me! "

And so it lay quite quiet, while the shots rattled through
the reeds and gun after gun was fired. At last, late in the
day, all was still; but the poor Duckling did not dare to rise
up; it waited several hours before it looked round, and then
hastened away out of the moor as fast as it could. It ran
on over field and meadow; there was such a storm raging
that it was difficult to get from one place to another.

Towards evening the Duckling came to a little miserable
peasant's hut. This hut was so dilapidated that it did not
itself know on which side it should fall; and that's why it
remained standing. The storm whistled round the Duckling
in such a way that the poor creature was obliged to sit
down, to stand against it; and the wind blew worse and
worse. Then the Duckling noticed that one of the hinges of
the door had given way, and the door hung so slanting that
the Duckling could slip through the crack into the room;
and that is what it did.

Here lived a woman, with her Cat and her Hen. And the
Cat, whom she called Sonnie, could arch his back and purr, he
could even give out sparks; but for that one had to stroke

his fur the wrong way. The Hen had quite little short legs, and therefore she was called Chickabiddy Shortshanks; she laid good eggs, and the woman loved her as her own child.

In the morning the strange Duckling was at once noticed, and the Cat began to purr and the Hen to cluck.

"What's this?" said the woman, and looked all round; but she could not see well, and therefore she thought the Duckling was a fat duck that had strayed. "This is a rare prize!" she said. "Now I shall have duck's eggs. I hope it is not a drake. We must try that."

And so the Duckling was admitted on trial for three weeks; but no eggs came. And the Cat was master of the house, and the Hen was the lady, and always said "We and the world!" for she thought they were half the world, and by far the better half. The Duckling thought one might have a different opinion, but the Hen would not allow it.

"Can you lay eggs?" she asked.

"No."

"Then will you hold your tongue!"

And the Cat said, "Can you curve your back, and purr, and give out sparks?"

"No."

"Then you will please have no opinion of your own when sensible folks are speaking."

And the Duckling sat in a corner and was melancholy; then the fresh air and the sunshine streamed in; and it was seized with such a strange longing to swim on the water, that it could not help telling the Hen of it.

"What are you thinking of?" cried the Hen. "You have nothing to do, that's why you have these fancies. Lay eggs, or purr, and they will pass over."

"But it is so charming to swim on the water!" said the Duckling, "so refreshing to let it close above one's head, and to dive down to the bottom."

"Yes, that must be a mighty pleasure, truly," quoth the

Hen. "I fancy you must have gone crazy. Ask the Cat about
it—he's the cleverest animal I know—ask him if he likes to
swim on the water, or to dive down: I won't speak about
myself. Ask our mistress, the old woman; no one in the world
is cleverer than she. Do you think she has any desire to swim,
and to let the water close above her head?"

"You don't understand me," said the Duckling.

"We don't understand you? Then pray who is to
understand you? You surely don't pretend to be cleverer
than the Cat and the woman—I won't say anything of
myself. Don't be conceited, child, and thank your Maker for
all the kindness you have received. Did you not get into a
warm room, and have you not fallen into company from
which you may learn something? But you are a chatterer,
and it is not pleasant to associate with you. You may believe
me, I speak for your good. I tell you disagreeable things, and
by that one may always know one's true friends! Only take
care that you learn to lay eggs, or to purr, and give out
sparks!"

"I think I will go out into the wide world," said the
Duckling.

"Yes, do go," replied the Hen.

And so the Duckling went away. It swam on the water,
and dived, but it was slighted by every creature because of
its ugliness.

Now came the autumn. The leaves in the forest turned
yellow and brown; the wind caught them so that they danced
about, and up in the air it was very cold. The clouds hung
low, heavy with hail and snowflakes, and on the fence stood
the raven, crying, "Croak! croak!" for mere cold; yes, it
was enough to make one feel cold to think of this. The poor
little Duckling certainly had not a good time. One evening—
the sun was just setting in his beauty—there came a whole
flock of great, handsome birds out of the bushes: they were
dazzlingly white, with long, flexible necks; they were swans.

They uttered a very peculiar cry, spread forth their glorious great wings, and flew away from that cold region to warmer lands, to fair open lakes. They mounted so high, so high! and the ugly Duckling felt quite strangely as it watched them. It turned round and round in the water like a wheel, stretched out its neck towards them, and uttered such a strange, loud cry as frightened itself. O! it could not forget those beautiful, happy birds; and so soon as it could see them no longer, it dived down to the very bottom, and when it came up again, it was quite beside itself. It knew not the name of those birds, and knew not whither they were flying; but it loved them more than it had ever loved any one. It was not at all envious of them. How could it think of wishing to possess such loveliness as they had? It would have been glad if only the ducks would have endured its company—the poor, ugly creature!

And the winter grew cold, very cold! The Duckling was forced to swim about in the water, to prevent the surface from freezing entirely; but every night the hole in which it swam about became smaller and smaller. It froze so hard that the icy covering cracked again; and the Duckling was obliged to use it continually to prevent the hole from freezing up. At last it became exhausted, and lay quite still, and thus froze fast into the ice.

Early in the morning a peasant came by, and when he saw what had happened, he took his wooden shoe, broke the ice-crust to pieces, and carried the Duckling home to his wife. Then it came to itself again. The children wanted to play with it; but the Duckling thought they wanted to hurt it, and in its terror fluttered up into the milk pan, so that the milk spurted down into the room. The woman clasped her hands, at which the Duckling flew down into the butter tub, and then into the meal barrel and out again. How it looked then! The woman screamed, and struck at it with the fire tongs; the children tumbled over one another in their efforts

to catch the Duckling; and they laughed and they screamed!
—well it was that the door stood open, and the poor creature
was able to slip out between the shrubs into the newly-fallen
snow—there it lay quite exhausted.

But it would be too melancholy if I were to tell all the
misery and care which the Duckling had to endure in the
hard winter. It lay out on the moor among the reeds, when
the sun began to shine again and the larks to sing: it was
a beautiful spring.

Then all at once the Duckling could flap its wings: they
beat the air more strongly than before, and bore it strongly
away; and before it well knew how all this happened, it
found itself in a great garden, where the elder trees smelled
sweet, and bent their long green branches down to the canal
that wound through the region. O, here it was so beautiful,
such a gladness of spring! and from the thicket came three
glorious white swans; they rustled their wings, and swam
lightly on the water. The Duckling knew the splendid
creatures, and felt oppressed by a peculiar sadness.

"I will fly away to them, to the royal birds! and they will
beat me, because I, that am so ugly, dare to come near them.
But it is all the same. Better to be killed by *them* than to be
pursued by ducks, and beaten by fowls, and pushed about
by the girl who takes care of the poultry yard, and to suffer
hunger in winter!" And it flew out into the water, and swam
towards the beautiful swans: these looked at it, and came
sailing down upon it with outspread wings. "Kill me!" said
the poor creature, and bent its head down upon the water,
expecting nothing but death. But what was this that it saw
in the clear water? It beheld its own image; and, lo! it was
no longer a clumsy dark-gray bird, ugly and hateful to look
at, but a—swan!

It matters nothing if one is born in a duck yard, if one
has only lain in a swan's egg.

It felt quite glad at all the need and misfortune it had

suffered, now it realized its happiness in all the splendor that surrounded it. And the great swans swam round it, and stroked it with their beaks.

Into the garden came little children, who threw bread and corn into the water; and the youngest cried, "There is a new one!" and the other children shouted joyously, "Yes, a new one has arrived!" And they clapped their hands and danced about, and ran to their father and mother; and bread and cake were thrown into the water; and they all said, "The new one is the most beautiful of all! so young and handsome!" and the old swans bowed their heads before him.

Then he felt quite ashamed, and hid his head under his wings, for he did not know what to do; he was so happy, and yet not at all proud. He thought how he had been persecuted and despised; and now he heard them saying that he was the most beautiful of all birds. Even the elder tree bent its branches straight down into the water before him, and the sun shone warm and mild. Then his wings rustled, he lifted his slender neck, and cried rejoicingly from the depths of his heart—

"I never dreamed of so much happiness when I was the Ugly Duckling!"

The poor little match girl stood alone in the freezing night, dreaming of her grandmother.

The Little Match Girl

It was terribly cold; it snowed and was already almost dark, and evening came on, the last evening of the year. In the cold and gloom a poor little girl, bareheaded and barefoot, was walking through the streets. When she left her own house she certainly had had slippers on; but of what use were they? They were very big slippers, and her mother had used them till then, so big were they. The little maid lost them as she slipped across the road, where two carriages were rattling by terribly fast. One slipper was not to be found again, and a boy had seized the other, and run away with it. He thought he could use it very well as a cradle, some day when he had children of his own. So now the little girl went with her little naked feet, which were quite red and blue with the cold. In an old apron she carried a number of matches, and a bundle of them in her hand. No one had bought anything of her all day, and no one had given her a farthing.

Shivering with cold and hunger she crept along, a picture of misery, poor little girl! The snowflakes covered her long fair hair, which fell in pretty curls over her neck; but she did not think of that now. In all the windows lights were shining, and there was a glorious smell of roast goose, for it was New Year's Eve. Yes, she thought of that!

In a corner formed by two houses, one of which projected

beyond the other, she sat down, cowering. She had drawn up her little feet, but she was still colder, and she did not dare to go home, for she had sold no matches, and did not bring a farthing of money. From her father she would certainly receive a beating, and besides, it was cold at home, for they had nothing over them but a roof through which the wind whistled, though the largest rents had been stopped with straw and rags.

Her little hands were almost numb with the cold. Ah! a match might do her good, if she could only draw one from the bundle, and rub it against the wall, and warm her hands at it. She drew one out. R-r-atch! how it sputtered and burned! It was a warm bright flame, like a little candle, when she held her hands over it; it was a wonderful little light! It really seemed to the little girl as if she sat before a great polished stove, with bright brass feet and a brass cover. How the fire burned! how comfortable it was! but the little flame went out, the stove vanished, and she had only the remains of the burned match in her hand.

A second was rubbed against the wall. It burned up, and when the light fell upon the wall it became transparent like a thin veil, and she could see through it into the room. On the table a snow-white cloth was spread; upon it stood a shining dinner service; the roast goose smoked gloriously, stuffed with apples and dried plums. And what was still more splendid to behold, the goose hopped down from the dish, and waddled along the floor, with a knife and fork in its breast, to the little girl. Then the match went out, and only the thick, damp, cold wall was before her. She lighted another match. Then she was sitting under a beautiful Christmas tree; it was greater and more ornamented than the one she had seen through the glass door at the rich merchant's. Thousands of candles burned upon the green branches, and colored pictures like those in the print shops looked down upon them. The little girl stretched forth her hand toward them; then the match went out. The Christmas lights mounted higher. She saw them now as stars in the sky: one of them fell down, forming a long line of fire.

"Now some one is dying," thought the little girl, for her old grandmother, the only person who had loved her, and who was now dead, had told her that when a star fell down a soul mounted up to God.

She rubbed another match against the wall; it became bright again, and in the brightness the old grandmother stood clear and shining, mild and lovely.

"Grandmother!" cried the child. "O! take me with you! I know you will go when the match is burned out. You will vanish like the warm fire, the warm food, and the great, glorious Christmas tree!"

And she hastily rubbed the whole bundle of matches, for she wished to hold her grandmother fast. And the matches burned with such a glow that it became brighter than in the middle of the day; grandmother had never been so large or so beautiful. She took the little girl in her arms, and both flew in brightness and joy above the earth, very, very high, and up there was neither cold, nor hunger, nor care—they were with God.

But in the corner, leaning against the wall, sat the poor girl with red cheeks and smiling mouth, frozen to death on the last evening of the Old Year. The New Year's sun rose upon a little corpse! The child sat there, stiff and cold, with the matches, of which one bundle was burned. "She wanted to warm herself," the people said. No one imagined what a beautiful thing she had seen, and in what glory she had gone in with her grandmother to the New Year's Day.

The Rags

At the door of a paper mill stood heaps of dust and rubbish, piled up into stacks; they had been gathered far and wide, and every rag in them had a tale to tell, and told it too; but we cannot listen to them all. Some of the rags were native, others came from foreign lands. Here now was a Danish rag, lying close to a rag from Norway; rank Danish was the one, and rank Norse the other; and there was likely to be some fun between the two, as any experienced Dane or Norseman could tell you.

They understood each other well enough, though the two languages were as different—so the Norwegian said—as French and Hebrew. "We go to the hillside for ours, and get it fresh from the fountainhead, while the Dane cooks up a mawkish, wishy-washy sort of a lingo."

The rags talked, and rags are rags all the world over; they are thought nothing of except in the dust heap.

"I am Norse," said the Norwegian; "and when I have said I am Norse, I guess I have said enough. I am firm of fiber, like the granite rocks of old Norway. The land there has a constitution, just like free America. It sets my fibers tickling to think of what I am, and to ring out my thoughts in words of the real old grit."

"But we have a complete literature," said the Danish rag; "do you understand what that is?"

"Understand!" repeated the Norwegian: "O this flatland creature! shall I give him a hoist uphill, and a Northern Light or two, clout as he is? When the Norway sun has thawed the ice, then come lubberly Danish hulks, bringing us butter and cheese, a right noble cargo; and they bring, too, by way of ballast, the Danish literature. We don't want it. One can do without stale beer in a land of sparkling springs, and up yonder is a natural well that was never bored; no, nor yet puffed into European notice by newsmongers, confederate jobbers, and bookmaking tourists in foreign parts. I speak free from the bottom of my lungs, and the Dane must get used to free sound; and so he will some day, in his Scandinavian clamber up our proud mountain land—that primary knob of the universe!"

"A Danish rag could never talk like that; no!" said the Dane. "It is not our nature: I know myself: and all our rags are like me. We are so good-natured, so unassuming. We only think too little of ourselves. Not that we gain much by our modesty: but I do like it; I consider it quite charming. Still I am perfectly aware of my own good qualities, I assure you, but I don't talk about them: nobody shall ever bring such a charge against me. I am gentle and complaisant; bear everything patiently, spite nobody, and speak good of all men—though there is not much good to be said of other people; but that is their business. I can afford to smile at it, I feel myself so much superior."

"Have done with this flatland drivel; it turns me sick," said the Norwegian, caught a puff of wind, and fluttered away from his own heap on to another.

Paper they both became, and, as chance would have it, the Norwegian rag became a sheet on which a Norseman wrote a true-love letter to a Danish girl; and the Danish rag became the manuscript for a Danish ode in honor of Norway's strength and beauty.

Something good there may come even of rags, when they are once out of the dust heap, and the change has been made in favor of truth and beauty; they keep up a good understanding between us, and in that there is a blessing.

The story is done. It is rather pretty, and offensive to nobody except to rags.

The Red Shoes

There was once a little girl. She was a tiny delicate little thing, but she always had to go about barefoot in summer, because she was very poor. In winter she had only a pair of heavy wooden shoes, and her ankles were terribly chafed.

An old mother shoemaker lived in the middle of the village, and she made a pair of little shoes out of some strips of red cloth. They were very clumsy, but they were made with the best intention, for the little girl was to have them. Her name was Karen.

These shoes were given to her, and she wore them for the first time on the day her mother was buried. They were certainly not mourning shoes, but she had no others, and so she walked barelegged in them behind the poor pine coffin.

Just then a big old carriage drove by, and a big old lady was seated in it. She looked at the little girl and felt very, very sorry for her, and said to the parson, "Give the little girl to me and I will look after her and be kind to her." Karen thought it was all because of the red shoes, but the old lady said they were hideous, and they were burnt. Karen was well and neatly dressed, and had to learn reading and sewing. People said she was pretty, but her mirror said, "You are more than pretty. You are lovely!"

At this time the Queen was taking a journey through the country, and she had her little daughter the Princess with her. The people, and among them Karen, crowded round the palace where they were staying, to see them. The little Princess stood at a window to show herself. She wore neither a train nor a golden crown, but she was dressed all in white with a beautiful pair of red morocco shoes. They were indeed a contrast to those the poor old mother shoemaker had made for Karen. Nothing in the world could be compared to these red shoes.

The time came when Karen was old enough to be confirmed. She had new clothes and she was also to have a pair of new shoes. The rich shoemaker in the town was to take the measure of her little foot. His shop was full of glass cases of the most charming shoes and shiny leather boots. They looked beautiful but the old lady could not see very well, so it gave her no pleasure to look at them. Among all the other shoes there was one pair of red shoes like those worn by the Princess. Oh, how pretty they were! The shoemaker told them that they had been made for an earl's daughter, but they had not fitted. "I suppose they are patent leather," said the old lady. "They are so shiny."

"Yes, they do shine," said Karen, who tried them on. They fitted and were bought, but the old lady had not the least idea that they were red, or she would never have allowed Karen to wear them for her confirmation. This she did however.

Everybody looked at her feet, and when she walked up the church to the chancel she thought that even the old pictures, those portraits of dead and gone priests and their wives, with stiff collars and long black clothes, fixed their eyes upon her shoes. She thought of nothing else when the minister laid his hand upon her head and spoke to her of holy baptism, the covenant of God, and said that henceforth she was to be a responsible Christian person. The solemn notes of the organ resounded, the children sang with their sweet voices, and the old precentor sang, but Karen thought only about her red shoes.

By the afternoon the old lady had been told on all sides that the shoes were red, and she said it was very naughty and most improper. For the future, whenever Karen went to the church she was to wear black shoes, even if they were old. Next Sunday there was holy communion, and Karen was to receive it for the first time. She looked at the black shoes and then at the red ones. Then she looked again at the red—and at last put them on.

It was beautiful sunny weather. Karen and the old lady went by the path through the cornfield, and it was rather dusty. By the church door stood an old soldier with a crutch. He had a curious long beard; it was more red than white—in fact it was almost red. He bent down to the ground and asked the old lady if he might dust her shoes. Karen put out her little foot too. " See what beautiful dancing shoes! " said the soldier. " Mind you stick fast when you dance." And as he spoke he struck the soles with his hand. The old lady gave the soldier a copper and went into the church with Karen. All the people in the church looked at Karen's red shoes, and all the portraits looked too. When Karen knelt at the altar rails and the chalice was put to her lips, she thought only of the red shoes. She seemed to see them floating before her eyes. She forgot to join in the hymn of praise, and she forgot to say the Lord's Prayer.

Now everybody left the church, and the old lady got into her carriage. Karen lifted her foot to get in after her, but just then the old soldier, who was still standing there, said, " See what pretty dancing shoes! " Karen couldn't help it: she took a few dancing steps, and when she began her feet continued to dance. It was just as if the shoes had a power over them. She danced right round the church. She couldn't stop. The coachman had to run after her, take hold of her, and lift her into the carriage; but her feet continued

Karen put on the red shoes, and suddenly her feet began to dance—and dance—and dance!

to dance, so that she kicked the poor lady horribly. At last they got the shoes off and her feet had a little rest.

When they got home the shoes were put away in a cupboard, but Karen could not help going to look at them.

The old lady became very ill. They said she could not live. She had to be carefully nursed and tended, and no one was nearer than Karen to do this. But there was to be a grand ball in the town and Karen was invited. She looked at the old lady, who after all could not live. Then she looked at the red shoes—she thought there was no harm in doing so. She put on the red shoes—that much she thought she might do—and then she went to the ball and began to dance. The shoes would not let her do what she liked: when she wanted to go to the right, they danced to the left. When she wanted to dance up the room, the shoes danced down the room, and then down the stairs, through the streets and out of the town gate. Away she danced, and away she had to dance, right away into the dark forest. Something shone up above the trees and she thought it was the moon, for it was a face, but it was the old soldier with the red beard. He nodded and said, " See what pretty dancing shoes! "

This frightened her terribly and she wanted to throw off the red shoes, but they stuck fast. She tore off her stockings, but the shoes had grown fast to her feet. So off she danced, and off she had to dance, over fields and meadows, in rain and sunshine, by day and by night, but at night it was fearful.

She danced into the open churchyard, but the dead did not join her dance; they had something much better to do. She wanted to sit down on a pauper's grave where the bitter wormwood grew, but there was no rest nor repose for her. When she danced towards the open church door, she saw an angel standing there in long white robes and wings which reached from his shoulders to the ground. His face was grave and stern, and in his hand he held a broad and shining sword.

" Dance you shall! " said he. " You shall dance in your red

shoes till you are pale and cold. Till your skin shrivels up
and you are a skeleton! You shall dance from door to door,
and wherever you find proud vain children, you must knock
at the door so that they may see you and fear you. Yea, you
shall dance— "

" Mercy! " shrieked Karen, but she did not hear the angel's
answer, for the shoes bore her through the gate into the fields,
and over roadways and paths. Ever and ever she was forced
to dance.

One morning she danced past a door she knew well. She
heard the sound of a hymn from within, and a coffin covered
with flowers was being carried out. Then she knew that the
old lady was dead, and it seemed to her that she was forsaken
by all the world and cursed by the holy angels of God.

On and ever on she danced. Dance she must, even through
the dark nights. The shoes bore her away over briars and
stubble till her feet were torn and bleeding. She danced away
over the heath till she came to a little lonely house. She knew
the executioner lived here, and she tapped with her fingers
on the window pane and said, " Come out! Come out! I can't
come in for I am dancing! "

The executioner said, " Don't you know who I am? I chop
the bad people's heads off, and I see that my ax is quivering."

"Don't chop my head off," said Karen, "for then I can
never repent of my sins. But pray, pray chop off my feet
with the red shoes! "

Then she confessed all her sins and the executioner
chopped off her feet with the red shoes, but the shoes danced
right away with the little feet into the depths of the forest.

Then he made her a pair of wooden feet and crutches,
and he taught her a psalm, the one penitents always sing.
And she kissed the hand which had wielded the ax and went
away over the heath.

"I have suffered enough for those red shoes! " said she.
"I will go to church now, so that they may see me." And

she went as fast as she could to the church door. When she got there, the red shoes danced right up in front of her, and she was frightened and went home again.

She was very sad all the week and shed many bitter tears, but when Sunday came she said, "Now then, I have suffered long enough. I should think I am quite as good as many who sit holding their heads so high in church."

She went along quite boldly, but she did not get further than the gate before she saw the red shoes dancing in front of her. She was more frightened than ever and turned back, this time with real repentance in her heart. Then she went to the parson's house and begged to be taken into service. She would be very industrious and work as hard as she could. She didn't care what wages they gave her, if only she might have a roof over her head and live among kind people. The parson's wife was sorry for her, and took her into her service. She proved to be very industrious and thoughtful. She sat very still and listened most attentively in the evening when the parson read the Bible. All the little ones were very fond of her, but when they chattered about finery and dress and about being as beautiful as a queen, she would shake her head.

Next Sunday they all went to church and they asked her if she would go with them, but she looked sadly, with tears in her eyes, at her crutches. And they went without her to hear the word of God, while she sat in her little room alone. It was only big enough for a bed and a chair. She sat there with her prayer book in her hand, and as she read it with a humble mind she heard the notes of the organ, borne from the church by the wind. She raised her tear-stained face and said, "Oh, God help me!"

Then the sun shone brightly round her, and the angel in the white robes whom she had seen that night at the church door stood before her. He no longer held the sharp sword in his hand but a beautiful green branch covered with roses.

He touched the ceiling with it and it rose to a great height, and wherever he touched it a golden star appeared. Then he touched the walls and they spread themselves out, and she saw and heard the organ. She saw the pictures of the old parsons and their wives. The congregation were all sitting in their seats singing aloud—for the church itself had come home to the poor girl in her narrow little chamber, or else she had been taken to it. She found herself on the bench with the other people from the parsonage. And when the hymn had come to an end, they looked up and nodded to her and said, " It was a good thing you came after all, little Karen! "

" It was through God's mercy! " she said. The organ sounded and the children's voices echoed so sweetly through the choir. The warm sunshine streamed brightly in through the window, right up to the bench where Karen sat. Her heart was so overfilled with the sunshine, with peace, and with joy, that it broke. Her soul flew with the sunshine to heaven, and no one there asked about the red shoes.

A Picture from the Castle Ramparts

It is autumn; we stand on the Castle Ramparts and look out across the sea with its many ships to the Swedish coast rising beyond, bright in the evening sunshine. Behind us the rampart descends abruptly; magnificent trees, whose yellow leaves are falling fast, grow below, and behind them are certain close-built, dull-looking houses with wooden palisades; a dreary walk has the sentinel who paces to and fro among them, but still drearier and darker must it be within those grated windows, for there dwell convict slaves, the worst of criminals.

A beam from the setting sun strays into the bare chamber, for the sun shines alike on the evil and on the good. The sullen, savage felon gazes gloomily on the cold sunbeam. A little bird flies upon the grating; his song, too, is for the evil as for the good. "Quirrevit!" his song is a brief one, but he remains perched on the grating; he flaps his wings, plumes his feathers, one tiny feather falls off, the others he ruffles up round his neck. And the chained criminal looks on, and a softer expression passes over his hard, coarse features, a feeling he is scarcely conscious of springs up within his heart, a feeling in some way akin to the sunbeam that has darted through the trellis, and the fragrance of the violets that in the spring cluster so abundantly outside his prison. But now sounds the horn of some home-bound huntsman;

clear, strong, and lively are the notes. Away from the grating flies the bird, from the bare wall fades away the sunbeam, and all is dark again within the chamber, dark again in the convict's heart. But, thank Heaven! the sun has shone therein, the bird's song has been heard, though but for one minute.

Die not away so soon, ye sweet, clear tones from the huntsman's horn! The evening is mild, the sea calm and smooth as a mirror.

A Vision of the Last Day

Of all the days of our life the greatest and most solemn is the day on which we die. Hast thou ever tried to realize that most sure, most portentous hour, the last hour we shall spend on earth?

There was a certain man, an upholder of truth and justice, a Christian man and orthodox, so the world esteemed him. And, in sooth, it may be that some good thing was found in him, since in sleep, amid the visions of the night, it pleased the Father of spirits to reveal him to himself, making manifest to him what he was in truth, namely, one of those who trust in themselves that they are righteous and despise others.

He went to rest, secure that his accounts were right with all men, that he had paid his dues and wrought good works that day; of the secret pride of his heart, of the harsh words that had passed his lips, he took no account at all. And so he slept, and in his sleep Death stood by his bedside, a glorious Angel, strong, spotless, beautiful, but unlike every other angel, stern, unsmiling, pitiless of aspect.

"Thine hour is come, and thou must follow me!" spake Death. And Death's cold finger touched the man's feet, whereupon they became like ice, then touched his forehead, then his heart. And the chain that bound the immortal soul to clay was riven asunder, and the soul was free to follow the Angel of Death.

But during those brief seconds, while yet that awful touch thrilled through feet, and head, and heart, there passed over the dying man, as in great, heaving ocean waves, the recollection of all that he had wrought and felt in his whole life; just as one shuddering glance into a whirlpool suffices to reveal in thought rapid as lightning, the entire unfathomable depth! just as in one momentary glance at the starry heavens we can conceive the infinite multitude of that glorious host of unknown orbs.

In such a retrospect the terrified sinner shrinks back into himself, and finding there no stay by which to cling, must feel shrinking into infinite nothingness; while the devout soul raises its thoughts to the Almighty, yielding itself up to Him in childlike trust, and praying, "Thy will be done in me!"

But this man had not the childlike mind, neither did he tremble like the sinner; his thoughts were still the self-praising thoughts in which he had fallen asleep. His path, he believed, must lead straight heavenward, and Mercy, the promised Mercy, would open to him the gates.

And, in his dream, the Soul followed the Angel of Death, though not without first casting one wistful glance at the couch where lay, in its white shroud, the lifeless image of clay, still, as it were, bearing the impress of the soul's own individuality. And now they hovered through the air, now glided along the ground. Was it a vast, decorated hall they were passing through, or a forest? It seemed hard to tell; Nature, it appeared, was formally set out for show, as in the artificial old French gardens, and amid its strange, carefully arranged scenes, passed and repassed troops of men and women, all clad as for a masquerade.

"Such is human life!" said the Angel of Death.

The figures seemed more or less disguised; those who swept by in the glories of velvet and gold were not all among the noblest or most dignified looking, neither were all those who wore the garb of poverty insignificant or vulgar. It was a

strange masquerade! But most strange it was to see how one
and all carefully concealed under their clothing something
they would not have others perceive, but in vain, for each
was bent upon discovering his neighbor's secret, and they
tore and snatched at one another till, now here, now there,
some part of an animal was revealed. In one was found the
grinning head of an ape, in another the cloven foot of a goat,
in a third the poison fang of a snake, in a fourth the clammy
fin of a fish.

All had in them some token of the animal—the animal
which is fast rooted in human nature, and which here was
seen struggling to burst forth. And, however closely a man
might hold his garment over it, the others would never rest
till they had rent the hiding veil, and all kept crying out,
"Look here! look now! here he is! there she is!"—and every
one mockingly laid bare his fellow's shame.

"And what was the animal in me?" inquired the disem-
bodied Soul; and the Angel of Death pointed to a haughty
form, around whose head shone a bright, wide-spread glory
of rainbow-colored rays, but at whose heart might be seen
lurking, half hidden, the feet of the peacock; the glory was,
in fact, merely the peacock's gaudy tail.

And as they passed on, large, foul-looking birds shrieked
out from the boughs of the trees; with clear, intelligible,
though harsh, human voices they shrieked, "Thou that
walkest with Death, dost remember me?" All the evil
thoughts and desires that had nestled within him from his
birth until his death now called after him, "Rememberest
thou me?"

And the Soul shuddered, recognizing the voices; it could
not deny knowledge of the evil thoughts and desires that
were now rising up in witness against it.

"In our flesh, in our evil nature, dwelleth no good thing,"
cried the Soul; "but, at least, thoughts never with me ripened
into actions; the world has not seen the evil fruit." And the

Soul hurried on to get free from the accusing voices; but
the great black fowls swept in circles round, and screamed
out their scandalous words louder and louder, as though
they would be heard all over the world. And the Soul fled
from them like the hunted stag, and at every step stumbled
against sharp flint stones that lay in the path. "How came
these sharp stones here? They look like mere withered leaves
lying on the ground."

"Every stone is for some incautious word thou hast spoken,
which lay as a stumbling block in thy neighbor's path, which
wounded thy neighbor's heart far more sorely and deeply
than these sharp flints now wound thy feet."

"Alas! I never once thought of that," sighed the Soul.

And those words of the Gospel rang through the air,
"Judge not, that ye be not judged."

"We have all sinned," said the Soul, recovering from its
momentary self-abasement. "I have kept the Law and the
Gospel, I have done what I could, I am not as others are!"

And in his dream this man now stood at the gates of
heaven, and the Angel who guarded the entrance inquired,
"Who art thou? Tell me thy faith, and show it to me in thy
works."

"I have faithfully kept the Commandments, I have humbled myself in the eyes of the world, I have preserved myself
free from the pollution of intercourse with sinners, I have
hated and persecuted evil, and those who practice it, and I
would do so still, yea, with fire and sword, had I the power."

"Then thou art one of Mohammed's followers?" said the
Angel.

"I? a Mohammedan?—never!"

"'He who strikes with the sword shall perish by the
sword,' thus spake the Son; His religion thou knowest not.
It may be that thou art one of the children of Israel, whose
maxim is, 'An eye for an eye, a tooth for a tooth,'—art thou
such?"

"I am a Christian."

"I see it not in thy faith or in thine actions. The law of Christ is the law of forgiveness, love, and mercy."

"Mercy!" The gracious echo of that sweet word thrilled through infinite space, the gates of heaven opened, and the Soul hovered toward the realms of endless bliss.

But the flood of light that streamed forth from within was so dazzlingly bright, so transcendently white and pure, that the Soul shrank back as from a two-edged sword, and the hymns and harp tones of Angels mingled in such exquisite celestial harmony as the earthly mind has not power either to conceive or to endure. And the Soul trembled and bowed itself deeper and deeper, and the heavenly light penetrated it through and through, and it felt to the quick, as it had never truly felt before, the burden of its own pride, cruelty, and sin.

"What I have done of good in the world, that did I because I could not otherwise, but the evil that I did—that was of myself!"

This confession was wrung from him; more and more the man felt dazzled and overpowered by the pure light of heaven; he seemed falling into a measureless abyss, the abyss of his own nakedness and unworthiness. Shrunk into himself, humbled, cast out, unripe for the kingdom of heaven, shuddering at the thought of the just and holy God—hardly dared he to gasp out, "Mercy!"

And the face of the Angel at the portal was turned toward him in softening pity. "Mercy is for them who implore it, not claim it; there is Mercy also for thee. Turn thee, child of man, turn thee back the way thou camest to thy clayey tabernacle; in pity is it given thee to dwell in dust yet a little while. Be no longer righteous in thine own eyes, copy Him who with patience endured the contradiction of sinners, strive and pray that thou mayest become poor in spirit, and so mayest thou yet inherit the Kingdom."

"Holy, loving, glorious forever shalt thou be, O, erring human spirit!"—thus rang the chorus of Angels. And again overpowered by those transcendent melodies, dazzled and blinded by that excess of purest light, the Soul again shrank back into itself. It seemed to be falling an infinite depth; the celestial music grew fainter and fainter, till common earthly sights and sounds dispelled the vision. The rays of the early morning sun falling full on his face, the cheerful crow of the vigilant cock, called the sleeper up to pray.

Inexpressibly humbled, yet thankful, he arose and knelt beside his bed. "Thou, who hast shown me to myself, help me now, that I may not only do justly, but love mercy, and walk humbly with my God. Thou, who hast convicted me of sin, now purify me, strengthen me, that, though ever unworthy of Thy presence, I may yet, supported by Thy love, dare to ascend into Thine everlasting light!"

The Vision was his; be the lesson, the prayer, also ours.

The Greenies

A rose tree stood in the window. Only a short time ago it was green and fresh, and now it looked sickly—no doubt it was in poor health. A whole regiment was quartered on it and was eating it up; but notwithstanding this greediness, the regiment was a very decent and respectable one. It wore bright green uniforms. I spoke to one of the "Greenies"; he was but three days old, and yet he was already a grandfather. Do you know what he said? It is all true—he spoke of himself and of the rest of the regiment. Listen!

"We are the most wonderful creatures in the world. We are engaged at a very early age, and immediately have the wedding. When the cold weather comes, we lay our eggs; the little ones lie snug and warm. The wisest of creatures, the ant (we have the greatest respect for him!) understands us. He appreciates us, you may be sure. He does not eat us up at once; he takes our eggs, lays them in the family ant hill, on the ground floor—lays them, labeled and numbered, side by side, layer on layer, so that each day a new one may creep out of the egg. Then he puts us in a stable, pinches our hind legs, and milks us till we die. He has given us the prettiest name—'Little milch-cow!'

"All creatures, who, like the ant, are gifted with common sense, call us so: it is only human beings who do not; they give us another name, and that we feel to be a great affront—

great enough to embitter our whole life. Could you not write a protest against it for us? could you not rouse these human beings to a sense of the wrong they do us? They look at us so stupidly, at times with such envious eyes, just because we eat a rose leaf, while they eat every created thing, all that is green and grows. O, they give us the most humiliating name! I will not even mention it. Ugh! I feel it in my stomach; I cannot even pronounce it—at least not when I have my uniform on, and I always wear that.

" I was born on a rose leaf. And the whole regiment live on the rose tree. We live off it, in fact; but then it lives again in us, who belong to the higher order of created beings. The human beings do not like us; they come and murder us with soapsuds—it is a horrid drink! I seem to smell it even now; it is dreadful to be washed when one was not made to be washed. Man! you who look at us with your severe soapsud eyes, think what our place in nature is: we are born on roses, we die in roses—our whole life is a poem. Do not give us the name which you yourself think most despicable, the name that I cannot bear to pronounce; call us the ants' milch-cows—the rose-tree regiment—the little green things."

And I—the man—stood looking at the tree, and at the little greenies—whose name I shall not mention, for I should not like to wound the feelings of one of the citizens of the rose tree, a large family with eggs and young ones—and at the soapsuds that I was going to wash them in, for I had come with soap and water, and murderous intentions; but now I will use it for soap bubbles. Look! how beautiful! perhaps there lies a fairy tale in each, and the bubble grows so large and radiant, and it looks as if there were a pearl lying inside of it!

The bubble swayed and swung, and flew to the door and then burst; but the door opened wide, and there stood Dame Fairy Tale herself! and now she will tell you better than

I can about—I won't say the name—the little green things.

"Tree-lice!" said Dame Fairy Tale. "One must call things by their right names; and if one may not do so always, one must at least have the privilege of doing so in fairy tales!"

The old woman told the man to put on her glasses, use her ear trumpet, and listen to all the potato had to tell!

What One Can Invent!

There was once a young man who wanted to become a poet. He wanted to be a poet by the next Easter, that he might marry and live by poetizing, and that, he knew, consisted merely in a knack of inventing, but then he never could invent! He was quite sure that he had been born too late; every subject had been taken before he came into the world, and there was nothing left for him to write about!

"What happy mortals were those who were born a thousand years ago," he sighed, "for then it was an easy matter to become immortal! Even those who were born but a hundred years ago were enviable; even at that time there was still something left to poetize about. But now all subjects are worn threadbare, and there is no use in my trying to write the nap on again!"

He thought and thought about it, till he grew quite thin and forlorn, poor fellow. No doctor could help him; there was but one who would be able to find the right remedy for him, and that was that wonderfully clever little old woman who lived in the little hut by the turnpike gate, that she opened and shut for all who passed that way. But she was wise and learned, and could open far more than the gate; she was much wiser than the doctor who drives in his carriage, and pays title taxes.

"I must go to her," said the young man. Her home was

small and tidy, but tiresome to look at—not a tree, not a
flower, grew anywhere near it. There was a beehive at the
door—very useful! There was a little potato field—very
useful! and a ditch with a blackthorn bush that had flowered,
and was bearing fruit—berries that draw your mouth together
if you eat of them before the frost has nipped them.

"What a picture all this is of our unpoetic time," thought
the young man. At least here was a thought, a grain of gold
dust that he found at the door of the little old woman's
cottage.

"Write that thought down," she said. "Crumbs are bread,
too. I know why you have come here; you cannot invent, and
yet you want to be a poet by next Easter!"

"Everything has been written about," he sighed; "our
time is not as the olden time."

"No, it is not," said the old woman. "In the olden time
such as I, who knew many weighty secrets, and how to cure
by the help of wonderful herbs, were burned alive; and in
the olden time, the poets went about with empty stomachs
and out at elbows. Ours is a very good time, the very best,
much better than the olden time; but your want of invention
all lies in your having no eyes to see with, and no ears to
hear, and you do not say your prayers of an evening. There
are any amount of things all around you that one might
poetize and write about, when one knows *how* to write
stories. You can find it in the earth where it grows and
sprouts; you can dip into the running or the stagnant water,
and you will find it there; but first of all, you must understand
the way of doing it—must know how to catch a ray of
sunshine. Now, just try my spectacles, put my ear trumpet
to your ear, say your prayers, and do, for once, leave off
thinking of yourself."

That last request was almost more than he could fulfill—
more than even such a wonderful old woman ought to ask.

He got the spectacles and the ear trumpet, and was put

out into the middle of the potato field; then she gave him a huge potato in his hand; presently he seemed to hear sounds in the potato, then came a song with words, a "story of everyday life," in ten volumes—but ten hills will do as well.

What was it the potato sang? It sang about itself and its ancestors, the arrival of the potato in Europe, and all it had had to suffer from suspicion and ill will before its value was recognized—before it was felt to be a much greater blessing than would be a lump of gold.

"We were distributed, by order of the King, at the court-house in every town; and there was issued a circular, setting forth our value and great merits, but no one believed it; they had not even the slightest idea how to plant us. One man dug a hole and threw his whole bushel of potatoes into it; another stuck them into the ground, one here, another there, and then waited for them to grow, and expected them to shoot up like trees that would bear potatoes, just as apple trees bear apples. There came buds, and stems, and flowers, and watery fruit, but it all withered away, and no one thought of the real blessing, the potato, that lay hidden under it all, in the ground. Yes, we have suffered much and been tried—that is, our forefathers have, but it all comes right in the end. Now you know our story."

"That's enough," said the old woman; "now look at the blackthorn."

"We, too," said the blackthorn, "have many relations in the land where the potatoes came from. A party of bold Norwegians from Norway steered their course westward through storm and fog till they came to an unknown country, where, under the ice and snow, they found herbs and grass, and bushes with blue-black berries of the vine—the blackthorn it was, whose berries ripen with the frost, and so do we. And that country they call 'Vineland,' and 'Greenland,' and 'Blackthorn Land.'"

"Why, that is quite a romantic story," said the young man.

"Now just follow me," said the little old woman, as she led him to the beehive. What life and movement there was! Then he looked in; there were bees standing in all the corridors, moving their wings like fans, so that there might be plenty of fresh air all through that large honey factory; that was their department. Then there were bees coming in from outside, from the sunshine and the flowers; they had been born with baskets on their legs; they brought the dust of the flowers and emptied it out of their little leg baskets; then it was sorted and worked up into honey and wax. Some came, some went; the queen of the hive wanted to fly, but when she flies, then all the others must fly too, and the right time for that had not yet come; but fly she would, and then to prevent her doing so, they bit her majesty's wings off—so that she was obliged to stay where she was.

"Now get up on the side of the ditch, where you can see all the town folk going past," said the little old woman.

"Goodness! what an endless number of people," said the young man. "One story after another! I seem to hear such buzzing and singing, and now it all grows quite confused! I feel quite dizzy—I shall fall!"

"No, don't," said the old woman—"don't fall backward; just go forward, right into the crowd of people; have eyes for all you see there, ears for all you hear, and above all, have a heart in it all! and before long you will be able to *invent*, and have thoughts for writing down—but before you go you must give me back my spectacles and my ear trumpet," and then she took both.

"Now I see nothing more," said the young man. "I do not even hear anything."

"In that case, it is quite impossible for you to be a poet by next Easter," said the old woman.

"But *when* shall I be a poet?" asked he.

"Neither by Easter nor by Whitsuntide! You have no knack at inventing," said she.

"But how then must I do, to get my living as by poetizing?"

"That I will tell you: write about those who have written. To hit their writings is to hit them. Don't let yourself be frightened; the more you do of such writing, the more you will earn, and you and your wife will be able to eat cake every day."

"What a trick *she* has at inventing," thought the young man, when he had thanked the old woman and bidden her good-bye. And he did as she had told him. Finding he could not be a poet himself, invent, and have bright ideas that people would talk of, he took to handling—and rather roughly—all those that were poets.

All this the little old woman has told me; she knows what one can invent!

It's Perfectly True!

"That's a terrible thing!" said a Hen; and she said it in a quarter of the town where the occurrence had not happened. "That's a terrible affair in the poultry house. I cannot sleep alone tonight! It is quite fortunate that there are many of us on the roost together!" And she told a tale, at which the feathers of the other birds stood on end, and the cock's comb fell down flat. It's perfectly true!

But we will begin at the beginning; and the beginning begins in a poultry house in another part of the town. The sun went down, and the fowls jumped up on their perch to roost. There was a Hen, with white feathers and short legs, who laid her right number of eggs, and was a respectable hen in every way; as she flew up on to the roost she pecked herself with her beak, and a little feather fell out.

"There it goes!" said she; "the more I peck myself the handsomer I grow!" And she said it quite merrily, for she was a joker among the hens, though, as I have said, she was very respectable; and then she went to sleep.

It was dark all around; hen sat by hen, but the one that sat next to the merry Hen did not sleep: she heard and she didn't hear, as one should do in this world if one wishes to live in quiet; but she could not refrain from telling it to her next neighbor.

"Did you hear what was said here just now? I name no

names; but here is a hen who wants to peck her feathers out to look well. If I were a cock I should despise her."

And just above the hens sat the Owl, with her husband and her little owlets; the family had sharp ears, and they all heard every word that the neighboring Hen had spoken, and they rolled their eyes, and the Mother-Owl clapped her wings and said.

"Don't listen to it! But I suppose you heard what was said there? I heard it with my own ears, and one must hear much before one's ears fall off. There is one among the fowls who has so completely forgotten what is becoming conduct in a hen that she pulls out all her feathers, and then lets the cock see her."

"*Prenez garde aux enfants*," said the Father-Owl. "That's not fit for the children to hear."

"I'll tell it to the neighbor owl; she's a very proper owl to associate with." And she flew away.

"Hoo! hoo! to-whoo!" they both screeched in front of the neighbor's dovecot to the doves within. "Have you heard it? Have you heard it? Hoo! hoo! there's a hen who has pulled out all her feathers for the sake of the cock. She'll die with cold, if she's not dead already."

"Coo! coo! Where, where?" cried the Pigeons.

"In the neighbor's poultry yard. I've as good as seen it myself. It's hardly proper to repeat the story, but it's quite true!"

"Believe it! believe every single word of it!" cooed the Pigeons, and they cooed down into their own poultry yard. "There's a hen, and some say that there are two of them that have plucked out all their feathers, that they may not look like the rest, and that they may attract the cock's attention. That's a bold game, for one may catch cold and die of a fever, and they are both dead."

"Wake up! Wake up!" crowed the Cock, and he flew up on to the plank; his eyes were still very heavy with sleep, but yet he crowed. "Three hens have died of an unfortunate attachment to a cock. They have plucked out all their feathers. That's a terrible story. I won't keep it to myself; let it travel farther."

"Let it travel farther!" piped the bats; and the fowls clucked and the cocks crowed, "Let it go farther! let it go farther!" And so the story traveled from poultry yard to poultry yard, and at last came back to the place from which it had gone forth.

"Five fowls," it was told, "have plucked out all their feathers to show which of them had become thinnest out of love to the cock; and then they have pecked each other, and fallen down dead, to the shame and disgrace of their families, and to the great loss of the proprietor."

And the Hen who had lost the little loose feather, of course did not know her own story again; and as she was a very respectable Hen, she said—

"I despise those fowls; but there are many of that sort. One ought not to hush up such a thing, and I shall do what I can that the story may get into the papers, and then it will be spread over all the country, and that will serve those fowls right, and their families too."

It was printed in the newspaper; and it's perfectly true— one little feather can easily become five hens.

There's a Difference

It was in the month of May; the wind was still cold, but trees and bushes, fields, and meadows, all proclaimed that spring was come. Flowers sprang forth everywhere, even the hedges were full of them, alive with them, one might say: it seemed as though they were the language wherein Spring announced herself, every single bright blossom a gladsome word of greeting. But the loveliest thing in the hedge was a little apple tree, and in that tree there was one bough especially fresh and blooming, completely weighed down by its wealth of delicate rosy buds, just ready to open. This bough was so lovely, it could not help knowing it, and therefore it was not one bit surprised when a grand carriage, passing along the road, stopped in front of it, and a young countess sitting in the carriage declared that of all the sweet, bright things of spring, that apple bough was the sweetest and brightest of all. And the apple bough was broken off, and the young countess held it in her own dainty hand, shading it from the sun with her silk parasol; and then they drove on to her home, a stately castle, full of lofty walls and decorated saloons; where gauzy white curtains fluttered at the open windows, and transparent vases stool full of beautiful flowers, and in one of these, which was carved as it were out of new-fallen snow, the apple bough was placed,

among fresh, light-green beech leaves, and a pretty sight it
was!

And so it came to pass that the apple bough grew proud,
quite like a human being.

All sorts of people passed through the rooms, and expressed
their admiration diversely; some said too much, some said
too little, some said nothing at all; and the apple bough
began to understand that there is a difference between human
beings as between vegetables. "Some are for use, some are
for ornament, and some could be dispensed with altogether,"
thought the apple bough. And as his position at the open
window commanded a view over gardens and meadows
below, he could look down upon all sorts of flowers and
plants, consider, and draw distinctions between them. They
stood beneath him all, some rich, some poor, some too poor.

"Miserable, rejected herbs!" snorted the apple bough. "It
is right and just that a distinction should be made—and yet
how unhappy they must feel, if indeed that sort of creature
is capable of feeling, like me and my equals; there is indeed
a difference, but it must be made, else all would be treated
as though they were alike." And the apple bough looked
down with especial compassion upon one kind of flowers
that grew in great multitudes upon the meadows and ditches;
no one gathered them for bouquets—they were too common,
they could be found springing up even between the paving
stones, they shot up everywhere, the rankest, most worthless
of weeds: they were dandelions, but the lower classes in
Denmark have given them the name of "Milk-pails."

"Poor despised outcasts!" went on the apple bough; "you
cannot help being what you are, so common! and with such
a vulgar name! But it is with vegetables as with men, there
must be a difference."

"A difference?" repeated the Sunbeam, as it kissed the
blossoming apple bough, and then flew on to kiss also the
golden "Milk-pails" out in the fields. And the Sunbeam's

sisters all did the same, kissing all the flowers equally, poor as well as rich.

Now the apple bough had never thought about our Lord's infinite love for all that lives and moves in Him, had never thought how much that is good and beautiful can lie hidden, but not forgotten. The apple bough had lived with human beings, and grown like them in this.

But the glorious Sunbeam knew better. "You are neither clear nor farsighted! What is this outcast herb that you are pitying so much?"

"The Milk-pails down there," replied the apple bough; "they are never tied up in bouquets, they are trodden under foot, there are too many of them; and when they run to seed they fly about in small bits of wool, and hang upon people's clothes. Weeds! weeds! but they must be as they are. I am really and truly grateful that I am not as one of them."

And now a whole troop of children roamed over the meadow, the youngest of them so tiny that he had to be carried by the others; and as he was now set down in the grass among the golden blossoms, he laughed for joy, kicked about with his short legs, rolled over and over, and plucked none but the yellow dandelions, which he kissed in his innocent delight. The bigger children busied themselves in breaking the flowers of the dandelions off from their hollow stalks, and joining these stalks into chains, first one for a necklace, then a longer chain to hang across the shoulders and round the waist, and last, a third for a circlet round the head; very soon they stood arrayed in splendid green chains. But the biggest of all the children carefully gathered the stalks bearing crowns of seed—that loose, aerial, woolly blossom, that wonderfully perfect ball of dainty white plumes; they held the white ball to their lips, trying to blow away all the white feathers with one puff of breath; whoever could do that would get new clothes before the year was out—so granny had told them. The poor despised herb was held as a prophet by this generation.

"Do you see now?" asked the Sunbeam; "don't you see its beauty and its power?"

"Yes, for children," replied the apple bough.

Presently came into the meadow an old woman. She stooped down and began digging for the dandelion roots with a blunt knife that had lost its handle. Some of the roots she would roast instead of coffee berries, others she would sell to the apothecary, who valued them as drugs.

"But beauty is something higher," protested the apple bough. "Only the chosen few can be admitted into the kingdom of the beautiful; there is a difference among plants as among men."

Then the Sunbeam spoke of the infinite love of the Creator for all His creatures, for all that has life, and His providence watching equally over all.

"Well, that is your opinion," replied the apple bough.

Some people now came into the room, among them the young countess who had placed the apple bough in the white vase by the window, and she carried in her hand something that was concealed by three or four large leaves held round it, lest a draught of air should injure it. Was it a flower? it was carried so carefully, more tenderly than the apple bough had been, when brought to the castle. Very gently the large leaves were removed, and behold the delicate globe of starry seeds borne by the despised dandelion plant! This it was which she had plucked so cautiously, carried so tenderly, lest one only of the dainty feathered arrows that help to round its globe-like form and sit so lightly, should be blown away. But it was quite perfect, not one seed was lost, and she admired so much the beautiful form, the airy lightness, the wondrous mechanism of a thing destined to be so soon scattered by the wind.

"Only see how wonderfully beautiful our Lord has made

it!" she said. "I will put it in a picture together with the apple bough: that is very lovely too; but this poor little weed is equally lovely, only in another way. Very different are they, and yet both are children in the kingdom of the beautiful."

And the Sunbeam kissed the poor weed, and then kissed the blossoming apple bough, whose delicate petal seemed to blush into a brighter red.

The Swan's Nest

Between the Baltic and the North Sea lies an old Swans' Nest—it is called Denmark; in it have been born, and will be born hereafter, Swans whose names shall never die.

In the olden time, a flock of Swans flew thence over the Alps to Milan's lovely green plains. There they lighted down and dwelt, for right pleasant was it there to dwell. These Swans were called Lombards.

Another flock, with bright shining plumage, and clear, truthful eyes, lighted down at Byzantium, nestled round the Emperor's throne, and spread out their broad white wings as shields to protect him. These were known as Varangians.

From the coasts of France arose a cry of anguish and terror—terror at the bloody Swans who, with fire under their wings, flew thither from the North. Loud was the prayer of village and town, "God save us from the wild Normans!"

On England's fresh meadow turf, near the shore, wearing a triple crown on his kingly head, his golden scepter stretching far over the land, stood the royal Swan, Canute the Dane.

And on Pomerania's shores the heathens bowed the knee, for thither, too, with drawn swords, and bearing the standard of the cross, had flown the Danish Swans.

"But this was in the days of old."

In times nearer our own, then, have mighty Swans been seen to fly out from the Nest. A flash of lightning cleft the air—lightning that shone over all Europe—for a Swan had flapped his strong wings and scattered the twilight mist, and the starry heavens became more visible—were brought, as it were, nearer the earth. The Swan's name was Tycho Brahe.

"Yes, just that once," it will be said; "but now, in our own generation?"

Well, in our own generation we have beheld Swans soaring in a high and glorious flight.

One we saw gently sweep his wings over the golden chords of the harp, whereupon sweet music thrilled through the northern lands, the wild Norwegian mountains lifted their proud crests higher in the full sunlight of the olden time, pine and birch bowed their heads and rustled their leaves, the "Gods of the North"—the heroes and noble women of Scandinavian history—lived and breathed again, their tall, stately figures standing out from the dark background of deep forests.

A second Swan we saw strike his pinions upon the hard marble rock till it cleft asunder, and new forms of beauty, hitherto shut up in the stone, were revealed to the light of day, and the nations of Europe gazed in wonder and admiration at the glorious statuary.

A third Swan we have seen weaving threads of thoughts that spun and spread around the earth, so that words can fly with lightning speed from land to land.

Dear to the protecting heavens above is the old Swans' Nest between the Baltic and the North Sea. Let mighty birds of prey, if they will, speed thither to tear it down. It shall not be! Even the unfledged, unplumed young ones will press forward to the margin of the Nest—we have seen it—will fight desperately with beak and claw, will offer their bleeding breast in defense of their home.

Centuries will pass away, and Swans will still fly forth from the Nest, and make themselves seen and heard far over the world; long will it be before the time shall come when in sad truth it may be said, "Behold the last Swan! Listen to the last sweet song from the Swans' Nest!"